Creatures of Habit

A Year in Cherrybrook

Book One: Spring

CHARLOTTE BROTHERS

I would like to thank my husband and children for encouraging me to indulge in my late-found passion for writing. I love each of you more than words can say.

Contents

Chapter One

A middle-aged man, every inch a gentleman farmer, knocked at the front door of his lifelong friend.

The heavy oak door was opened by the aged butler, whose somewhat wooden expression relaxed a modicum when he saw who stood before him. "Good afternoon, sir."

"Good afternoon, Dobson," said the visitor, removing his hat and taking advantage of the iron boot scraper. When he felt free of spring mud, he looked up again.

Dobson, who had been patiently waiting, said with particular gravity, "The elder Mr. Trellaway is expecting you, sir."

"He is, is he?" replied Mr. Merritt with a curious lift of an eyebrow. He had not failed to comprehend the significance of Dobson's clarification.

"I believe he is in his study, sir," said Dobson, bowing stiffly as he stood to the side, allowing Mr. Gregory Merritt to pass.

"I will see myself through the house," said Mr. Merritt with a quick nod to the elderly manservant. "No need to trouble yourself," and he started off in haste to find his friend.

Before Mr. Merritt reached the end of the hall, Trellaway's study door was thrown open and his host popped out. Albert smiled broadly and waved his spectacles wildly before tucking them into the breast pocket of his amply padded, light tweed vest as he ushered in his friend.

"You may have guessed my news?" asked Mr. Trellaway, rubbing his hands together gleefully and gently pushing his visitor into a soft chair. Without leaving time for an answer, he rushed on. "Of course, you have," he winked, "Lawrence has returned at last! And with honours too, the young rascal! He was made a lieutenant... but we all knew that from his letters."

"Where is he?! May I see him?" asked Mr. Merritt, starting up from the chair only to have a restraining hand put upon his chest.

"You will have to come again soon to see him, for Lawrie is out for a walk with Lucy and Charles. Getting reacquainted with the–"

"Get to the point, Trellaway! What about the injury?!" Mr. Merritt leaned forward eagerly and held out his hand in a gesture of anticipation. "He is out for a walk, you say?"

"You remember he wrote to tell us not to worry ourselves, but you understood how it was. The missus and I braced for the worst, but —". Trellaway didn't finish his sentence. Perhaps seeing that his friend could no longer bear the suspense, the happy father's face broke into a grin, and he held his arms out wide and said, "No cause for alarm in the least! Lawrie is quite recovered." He lowered himself into his worn chair across from his guest. "Barely a limp. Hardly noticeable." Sitting back comfortably and folding his hands over his stomach, he confided, "If Lawrence has far to walk, he uses a walking stick. It galls him to need it, but his mother and I are convinced he is overly conscious of it.

"No question that the boy is happy to be home." Trellaway gazed at a spot just above Mr. Merritt's head. "Now," he smiled mistily, "all that is left for us to do is arrange a wedding!" He nodded appreciatively, as though he could already see Lawrence and Eugenia at the altar.

Mr. Merritt grunted and took out his handkerchief to wipe his brow. He saw that it was time to pull Trellaway back down to solid ground.

He began by a sonorous clearing of his throat. "As much as we've planned for this occasion, Trellaway, we cannot force them together. Instead, you must see first which way the wind blows with Lawrie. If he lacks enthusiasm for our suggestion, do not panic," Merritt shook a sagacious forefinger. "These things take time, and I must warn you that Eugenia has grown very independent of late. If our children will suit, it will have to be their doing, or at least they will have to believe it to be." He scooted forward in the leather chair and said with conviction, "They are part of this new breed of young people who demand some sort of romantic sensibility."

A comfortable and somewhat rambling conversation followed, during which various means of reintroducing their grown children to each other were discussed. Finally, an intimate family evening party was agreed upon, and the two country gentlemen shook hands warmly in the front garden. Mr. Trellaway spun on his heels and returned to his study, smiling, and Mr. Merritt whistled a little ditty and walked up the road in the direction of home.

Eugenia Merritt was in the garden. Dressed in her well-worn jonquil morning dress, she blew at an errant tendril of blond hair that was tickling her nose as she crouched forward to snip off spent narcissi blooms. How pleasing was the slicing sound of the garden clippers, she thought, and how sweetly the birds did sing as they rustled and chirped in the hedgerow along the garden wall behind her.

She hummed a little and said as she snipped, "Lovelies, I am sorry to say it, but you are no longer in your prime. You have done your best, however, which is all any of us can do."

Next, she selected an assortment of the best April had to offer, some of the freshly budded daffodils and fragrant hyacinths and laid them gently in the shallow basket beside her.

Near the basket lay an old grey and black mongrel dog. Its ancestry unknown, and pedigree doubtful, he wore about his neck a very fine collar with a smart red bow. This former stray bore the unlikely name of 'Mister Cavendish'. Mister Cavendish cocked his head as she spoke, but when he did not detect his name in her chatter, he rested his head again upon his paws and waited patiently, his faithful gaze following her every movement.

Before returning to the house, Eugenia made her way into the kitchen garden and selected a small radish and some dandelion greens. Some days ago, she had found a young, injured rabbit and it was now convalescing in a small hutch next to the back door, its right hind foot still nearly useless. Eugenia had half a mind to release the rabbit into the garden and let nature take its course, but there was the likely possibility that the vegetables would suffer.

With a sigh, she carried the basket of cut flowers, the radish, and greens up the central gravel walk, stopped to give the little caged rabbit its portion, and then continued into the house with Mister Cavendish trotting at her heels.

After changing her dress for tea, Eugenia arrived in the breakfast room and discovered her parents were already seated at the table. Their animated conversation ceased abruptly as she entered the room and they exchanged glances. Eugenia paused momentarily in the doorway, and her eyes darted from one to the other with a questioning look.

There could be nothing seriously amiss, she decided, because both her father and mother were smiling broadly. However, her father was a steady man and an indulgent father, not given to frequent out-bursts of strong feeling, so a shadow crossed Eugenia's face when she saw that he seemed to be decidedly on the jump. He stood clumsily at her approach, his knee striking the leg of the table which caused a minor tremor amongst the cups and saucers.

Her mother fingered her brooch nervously and said, "Come. Sit down, dear." There was a bit more blush to her mother's cheeks than usual, and a bit too much brightness in her blue eyes. A cheerful (if sometimes nervous) woman, her mother was usually in harmony with her husband. Their felicitous marriage should have resulted in a large family, but sadly the other children born to this happy union had died in infancy. This meant, of course, that Eugenia had not only enjoyed a degree of agency often denied daughters of comfortable country gentry, but also their full concern and attention.

Eugenia sat at the table and reached for a bun. There it was again! Her parents had distinctly exchanged meaningful glances. Something of significance had occurred.

One second more, and she had a sinking feeling that she knew what that something or someone was. The fighting in Spain had ended in a hard-won victory and now young men were steadily returning to their families. It must be that *he* had returned.

Eugenia's neighbours and friends had been announcing betrothals and enjoying flirtations in recent years, Eugenia's parents had the out-modish notion that she should reserve herself for the eldest son of their dearest friends, the Trellaways. It was the only circumstance that defied logic in otherwise so reasonable a household. Her parents were positively mulish about it! Not that she minded missing some of the parties and dances that more marriage-minded mothers put on. She was so happily situated that, other than the sort of pang she felt at being left out of something exciting and romantic, she doubted any man would regard the freedom and unladylike interests that her parents, her father in particular, had allowed.

Lawrence Trellaway was several years her senior and whilst they had played together as children, he had been a timid boy. She'd thought him too serious and rather boring. Besides, the awkwardness of knowing how their parents felt about them made affection of any kind impossible; at least that is how Eugenia had felt. They had hardly spoken during those last years leading up to his military duty.

Her parents would not, they had promised, force her to marry Lawrie. But nor would they permit a serious flirtation or consider any offers made to her before he returned from service to court her; as if he would certainly do so!

After a few minutes of strained silence, it did not come as a surprise to Eugenia when her mother casually suggested that she and Eugenia visit the dressmaker.

"Of course, I shall not," disagreed Eugenia in the most agreeable way possible. She smiled sweetly at her mamma and said, "I prefer to ask Miss Lyle to make my dresses."

"Well, have it your way," replied her mother without hesitation. She did not appear the least put out by Eugenia's obstinacy. "The girl does have a way with sewing. Perhaps today you can discover whether or not she can meet us at the drapers before the week is over."

Since it seemed that Mrs. Merritt was content to offer no further details and was now very much concerned with levelling the butter on her pastry, Eugenia asked "Is there any particular reason that I so urgently need a new gown, Mother?"

Instead of answering, Mrs. Merritt popped the small wedge of buttered bun in her mouth and held up her napkin to show that she was unable to answer until she was done chewing. She glanced toward her husband, however, who cleared his throat and looked meditatively at Eugenia.

"You might be the first young lady to regard the offer of a new gown with such suspicion, m'dear."

Eugenia opted to remain politely silent in hope of drawing him out. She carefully sipped her tea and tried to act as though she had quantities of both time and patience. She smiled gently, but inside she knew it was all she could do to keep from blurting out, "It is Lawrie, isn't it? He has come back from the war," but she held her silence and blinked innocently at her father.

"Your mother and I have agreed that we ought to host a small party."

"A small party," repeated Eugenia mechanically.

She began to protest, but her father held up his hand and declared that she could hardly object to a small party of charades and cards. "There is nothing so commonplace as that," he said.

Her mother, evidently finished chewing, laid down her napkin. "And you must invite Miss Lyle. Her company will put you at ease."

"Why will I need to be made easy at a commonplace evening in my own home with my closest friend?"

Her father answered, "Lawrence has returned home, and we want to do our part in welcoming him. Your mother and I think it is not too much to ask of you to behave prettily."

While her parents exchanged looks of triumph, Eugenia scowled and sneaked a scrap of warm buttered bread down to Mister Cavendish who was resting his head in her lap beneath the table. Under his furry eyebrows, his eyes rolled up to look at his mistress with an expression, Eugenia was sure, of sympathetic misery.

On the very same day in the very same hour, in the home of the Trellaway family, a very similar conversation was taking place.

Lawrence was tapping his teacup with a spoon while staring down at his half-eaten plum cake. Charles and Lucy, his younger brother and sister, were slumped in their chairs, smirking, but today it went unnoticed by Mr. and Mrs. Trellaway. His father had finally taken a breath after extolling the many virtues of Miss Eugenia Merritt, whom Lawrie clearly remembered as a rather bossy, headstrong girl with tangled, fair hair and mucking boots, always toting around some half-starved, sick bird or small mammal.

He grudgingly allowed that she might have changed during the intervening years. He certainly had.

It seemed like a lifetime ago, his childhood before the war. He had been a different person then, a mere lad. Soft. Gutless. Now his own brother and sister said that they should hardly have known him if they had not been expecting his return. He was no taller, of course (still of modest height at best), but his hair had lightened to a soft, sandy blond, and his skin was tanned from the daily exposure to the Mediterranean sunshine. His muscles were strong, used to strenuous exercise. He also sported several nasty scars under his shirt and breeches, but they didn't signify. What did signify, however, was the limp.

His thoughts were interrupted by his father's demanding intonation and his sister's tittering laughter.

"I shall take your silence as willingness, then?"

Lawrence sat up quickly. "What do you assume I have agreed to, sir?"

"Why, to offer for Eugenia! It is the fondest wish of both Mr. Merritt and I. Oh! And your dear mother, of course." Here he reached over to squeeze his wife's hand, smiling at her warmly. "Isn't that right, my treasure?"

When Lawrence looked at his mother questioningly, she nodded happily, and her lace cap jiggled atop her head. Another stifled giggle came from the end of the table where his sister sat and Lawrie pinned Lucy with a glare, hoping to squelch her mirth at his obvious discomfiture. When she had finished her obnoxious outburst, Lawrie blinked slowly, and focused his gaze upon his father once again. With a smile, he said, "I cannot possibly propose marriage to a girl to whom I have not spoken since schoolroom days, and I cannot believe that she would appreciate such an impudent offer. I don't suppose that you have asked the lady in question on my behalf?"

Lawrie intended this as a jest, but grew alarmed when, instead of an indignant refusal, his mother glanced aside to his father and answered with some hesitation, "Well, my dear.... not .... not precisely."

Lawrence did not wish to be disrespectful, but his jaw slackened in surprise, and he let his spoon clatter to rest on the tea plate.

His father said, "Don't be foolish. I would do no such thing." Then he leaned in closer, man to man, as if a little clarification was all it would require to remove the note of hysteria that had crept into the teatime conversation. Mr. Trellaway patted his son on the shoulder and smiled sagely, "Put it from your mind. Maybe after you renew your acquaintance with Miss Merritt you will change your mind. One could never say she was dull, good heavens, no! But she may be plain. Perhaps you'd like to see her and judge for yourself, eh? No need to take our word on it. Your mother and I are hardly impartial in the matter, I know. The point is this," he said conspiratorially, leaning closer and jabbing his son's shoulder, "if you want to see Eugenia, all you need to do is watch the road from the parlour window at a quarter past two on Wednesdays or Mondays. She walks uptown then, with a maid or her father and her little dog."

At this ridiculously precise description of a young lady's weekly destination, Lawrie stopped his hand just as he was about to take up his spoon again from the small white and blue plate.

"And how would you know this, sir?"

His father smiled again, "You forget that here in Cherrybrook we are creatures of habit. Unless disaster strikes, we are content with our usual way of doing things."

"Perhaps Lawrence isn't lonely, dear husband," said Mrs. Trellaway. "We ought to leave him alone. Some men, you know, never tire of a bed on the hard ground, the sway of a ship, the changing of horses and posting house meals."

Lawrie regarded his mother with suspicion but said politely, "May we please change the subject?"

"Of course, dearest," replied his mother sweetly.

When Wednesday came, Lawrence stubbornly avoided all front-facing windows at the hour at which Eugenia Merritt was expected to stroll by on her merry way. Thankfully, not another word was spoken about it, and Lawrence began to relax into country life once again.

Even though he had been happy enough to leave home when the time came, any doubt he might have had then, surrounding his future, had dissipated. He realised during the fighting that he wanted nothing more than to return home and ride through his fields, pick ripe fruit from his own trees, and fish in the lake and local streams; to re-inhabit all those places that he had loved for as long as he could remember. He was also ready to take on the work his father had for him and continue to maintain and develop the family home, gardens, and farm.

Now that he was back, the simple delights of Cherrybrook meant more to him than ever. He was not strictly hiding from the people he had known all his life, but nor was he going out of his way to be seen, for he did not want to arouse curious gazes and questions about his faltering gait. Instead, during the day, he pottered about in the garden, and went riding or fishing. If it was raining, he might read with a glass of claret in hand or play cards with his brother and sister. When the evening was fine, Lawrie enjoyed a solitary walk. There were plenty of paths to reacquaint himself with on Trellaway land and, when he felt like it, he walked the road that wound lazily in the direction of the neighbouring town of Wellsey.

With all the quietness, the cleanliness, and the fresh air of home, he finally felt that the war truly was over and the life he had fought to protect did, indeed, remain.

So far, Lawrence had avoided going down the road past the Merritt house. It was only a matter of time, of course, before he would have to face Eugenia and her family. Already his mother was talking about an evening of cards in the near future, so there was no need to hasten the event or excite Mr. or Mrs. Merritt by appearing outside their house. What a pity that the best trout fishing was in a lake just beyond the Merritts' property! It was a small lake that used to be blessed with an abundance of well-grown trout (unless the local lads had fished it dry while he was away). Soon enough, he'd brave that patch of road with his friend and battalion companion, Captain John Fortescue. Fortescue was due to arrive on the morrow, and there was no way that Lawrie was going to give up the opportunity of prime fishing, husband-hunting women notwithstanding.

Fortescue had a way of enchanting people, making them laugh and forget their worries and pains. The captain was everything that Lawrie was not, tall and lanky with natural social grace and wit. His dark hair fell effortlessly into those careless waves that seemed to please ladies of all ages, and his fine teeth, sparkling eyes, and wolfish grin did nothing to detract from his considerable charm.

Therefore, it came as no surprise to Lawrence that, when the captain arrived, his friend had so thoroughly enthralled his younger siblings by the end of the second day, that they hung upon every word of his stories. Lucy and Charles listened just as hungrily as those lonely and frightened lads had, hunkered down in the war camps of Spain.

On Monday afternoon, Lawrie decided they had exhausted the stream fishing and it was now time to take Fortescue to the lake. As he and John were walking with rods in hand, bait, and bucket, John broke off talking abruptly and nudged Lawrence. They were just about to pass a sturdy housemaid and her very fine-looking mistress. The young lady was fresh-faced and flushed. Her eyes matched her dress, as blue as bluebells. Beneath her straw bonnet peeked some blonde curls. She held a leash in her hand and was walking a scraggly little terrier wearing a canary yellow bow about its neck.

Both men did their best to bow and lift their hats while holding their tackle and Lawrie, his walking stick, but their efforts must have appeared comical. They were rewarded by a curious but warm, dimpled smile from the young lady, a scowl from her formidable maid and a bark from the small dog.

John, fast to find his tongue, said "Enjoy your walk, Miss."

The girl smiled and nodded but said nothing. Then she tugged at the dog's leash and marched on toward town without looking back.

Even though Lawrie couldn't have begun to describe what Eugenia looked like based on memories of her, he felt certain that the young lady with the prettified mongrel was indeed the Merritts' daughter.

John, had stopped in place and been in the middle of saying "What a dashed pretty girl! Do you know–" when he must have noticed something arresting in Lawrie's expression so broke off his sentence and said instead, "What is it, Trellaway?"

"Unless I am mistaken - and I am quite sure I am not - that young woman is the very one my frightfully old-fashioned parents want me to marry! They wasted no time in reminding me of her practically the moment I walked through the door."

"Ah! Most excellent parents!" jibed John with a grin, half turning around for another look at the lady. "I am surprised you want to spend any time at all with me when such an enchanting creature lives nearby."

Lawrie adjusted the position of his fishing rod and began walking again. "Miss Merritt and I have grown up as neighbours, our parents have been fast friends our entire lives, and somehow, they have got it fixed in their heads that we are perfect for one another."

John arched an eyebrow. "And are you?" he asked.

Lawrence just laughed and said with a shrug, "I am quite sure we used to be a trial to one another when we were children. Today is the first I have seen her in years. Anyway," Lawrie said lightly, "it is a foolish notion on the part of our parents you must allow."

"I tell you what, Trellaway, if you have no intention of throwing yourself under for her, I shall be happy to provide your Miss Merritt a diversion. Oh, not a slip on the shoulder, nothing shabby; but solicitous I *will* be. It will be my pleasure, and who can say? Perhaps your lady will capture my heart." John slapped Lawrie's back good-naturedly. "Anyway, with all good luck, you will be free of an obligatory proposal. How's that?"

"Wonderful" said Lawrence, but he wasn't sure it was wonderful, for the hoyden Eugenia was now a very attractive lady.

Chapter Two

In due course, Eugenia's new spring gown was finished and the evening arrived upon which Mr. and Mrs. Merritt had settled for an evening of cards with their old friends.

An invitation had been extended to the entire Trellaway family, the newly arrived Captain Fortescue, and Marian, the vicar's daughter and Eugenia's close friend.

Marian had arrived early, as planned, to dress with Eugenia.

"Are you not nervous?" enquired Marian for the third time.

"Certainly, I am, or I would not have asked you to come early."

"Well, you do not appear nervous. That's a good thing. I should be all a-quiver if it were me!"

"Mr. Trellaway has a guest with him," said Eugenia wickedly. "I believe you ought to be nervous. Heavens! What if Lieutenant Trellaway's friend, Captain Fortescue, is a very appropriate sort of match for you?"

"Eugenia! Why did you go and say that? Now look at me. I am trembling, and you the very picture of serenity. It is too unfair!" Both girls laughed and then got down to the business of dressing. Eugenia's new gown of periwinkle blue fitted her perfectly, and she arched her back and twisted this way and that in front of the mirror before turning with a grateful smile to Marian.

"It is lovely! You have outdone yourself once more." With one final admiring glance at her reflection, Eugenia turned and said, "Now, let me help you."

She watched as Marian stepped into her gown, one of mossy green that set off her hazel eyes admirably, and Eugenia moved around her friend's back to help her fasten it.

Marian asked casually, "Have you seen Mr. Trellaway? Since he's come home, I mean?"

Eugenia stopped her buttoning for a moment and then resumed. "I believe I did. Last week when Mary and I were walking we passed two gentlemen out for a day's fishing. While we passed them swiftly and did not spare more than a glance, I am convinced that they were none other than Mr. Trellaway and his friend."

"Well?" Marian asked eagerly, "What were they like?"

"Lawr- Mr. Trellaway was much changed," said Eugenia thoughtfully. "This Mr. Trellaway was seasoned-looking and his hair a much lighter colour. His features were the same as I remember, a rather small, straight mouth, a nicely shaped nose, neither too large nor small, and soft blue eyes. Still," she said, reaching the final button, "I am not perfectly certain it was him, for it was the briefest of moments and I 'twas not about to stare so I am not prepared to swear upon it, mind you."

"You should never swear, Eugenia, no matter your strength of feeling."

Eugenia grinned and rolled her eyes, but since she was behind her friend, Marian was spared the irreverent response to her admonition.

"Anyway, the gentleman walking with the presumed Mr. Trellaway was very smart! He was quite a cut above any of the young men here. He was tall and dark-haired, with pleasing features and something sparkling about him. He looked not exactly dangerous, but exciting. Good humoured, I imagine. You might like him."

"I might like him? It sounds as though you are already predisposed to liking him very much yourself!"

"Perhaps I am," said Eugenia with a light laugh.

It was an hour later when the pair of young ladies descended the stairs and peeked into the parlour. Several large vases of freshly cut flowers and foliage that Eugenia had arranged that afternoon were set about the room on tables.

Against the wall on the left was a sideboard with glasses and cups for punch and tea, as well as bread and cheese, cold cut meats and fruit. The soft chairs and settee had been moved into a horseshoe formation, cleared in the centre to allow for a game of charades, and a table with lit candles was in the far end of the room, with a fresh deck of cards at the ready.

As the girls stood admiring the decorations, they both jumped as a loud knock sounded, followed by Mister Cavendish's excited barks. Mr. Merritt went hurtling by the open parlour door nearly blundering into Eugenia and Marian in his eagerness to greet their guests. The girls exchanged amused glances and after a pause, followed in Mr. Merritt's wake.

"Mr. and Mrs. Trellaway! Welcome!" beamed Mr. Merritt at Lawrie's parents. "You know the way in, of course."

"Hart," said Mr. Merritt to their butler, "please show our good friends through. And who have we here? Ah, the youngest Trellaways! Come in Lucy, Charles. I hope you're ready for a good game or two, yes?"

The children nodded politely and entered on their parents' heels. Next came Lawrie and Fortescue, bringing up the rear. They each shook hands with Mr. Merritt, and Mr. Merritt grasped Lawrie hard by the shoulder in his exuberance, saying "Come in! Come in! We are delighted to have you back. Delighted!" Mr. Merritt continued. "And you must be Captain Fortescue? Pleased to make your acquaintance, sir. May I present my wife, Mrs. Merritt, and our daughter, Miss Merritt and her friend, Miss Lyle? Do come in and make yourself comfortable."

Lawrence noticed Eugenia meet his gaze with a friendly but appraising one of her own before turning her attention to Fortescue. Miss Lyle smiled sweetly. She seemed very little changed from what he remembered of her.

Lawrie bowed and smiled politely, but Fortescue, who knew the importance of creating a good first impression when presenting himself to young ladies, swept a bow with practised grace. Lawrie reached a finger inside his collar to loosen his cravat, which suddenly felt tight, as he watched the girls' eyes widen in sparkling appreciation of Fortescue's dashing gesture.

Mrs. Merritt drew near Lawrence, touching his arm, and Lawrie smiled respectfully at his hostess, allowing her to pull him deeper into the front hall.

"It has been such a long time, Lawrence," she said softly. "You are quite grown up! I should not have recognized you but for your gentle manner. Always the quiet yet observant young man you were. I see that in that regard, you remain the same. Come and tell Hart what he might pour for you."

Lawrence held out his arm for Mrs. Merritt and led her to the parlour behind Fortescue, who had Miss Marian on one elbow and Miss Merritt on the other.

The evening proved to be lively. The Merritts and the Trellaways were fond of jokes and laughter and, if not everyone in the room was wholly comfortable, it went undetected by the majority.

Lawrie supposed his own awkwardness to stem from this being the first proper re-introduction to civil society and the presence of Miss Merritt. He knew he was distracted and self-conscious, which caused him to stumble in his games. No matter who he was paired with, the results were dismal, but they were especially dire whenever Eugenia was his partner.

What made it worse was that Eugenia seemed to notice. She was sitting across from him, and they had just lost the last set. She smiled and said pityingly, "Well, perhaps we ought to change our seats sand try a new set with new partners?" Then, Eugenia rose from her chair and announced her intention of seeking a quick refreshment before they were to begin again.

Hastily, the young men stood and bowed slightly.

Lawrence watched Eugenia sweep her way across the room to the punch bowl, with her little dog trotting behind her. Turning back to the table, he saw that Fortescue had also been watching Eugenia, with quite a different expression on his face, and one he'd seen on his friend's face before. Lawrie gave a slight cough which succeeded in breaking Fortescue's stare.

Out of the corner of his eye, he noticed Miss Lyle biting her lip nervously. She looked flushed. She might be thirsty, or perhaps she had noticed the way that Fortescue's gaze so willingly followed her friend. Lawrie silently chastised himself for his lack of manners and smiled at the vicar's daughter.

"May I bring you a lemonade, Miss Lyle?" he asked.

"Oh yes, please!" she replied with bashful enthusiasm.

Lawrence crossed the room and was just about to step up to the sideboard when Eugenia spun around to return to the game table. Apparently surprised to find him at her elbow, she spilled the contents of her glass onto the front of her dress.

"Please! Allow me- I am so sorry-" Lawrie started to say as he pulled out his handkerchief and started toward her with the cotton in his hand. He froze mid-action. He could not jolly well help her dry her bosom.

Eugenia took the proffered handkerchief from his outstretched hand and thanked him. She turned her back to him and bent her head and scrubbed at the front bodice of her gown. Lawrie found himself staring at the nape of her shapely neck.

She turned again suddenly. "May I return this later?"

"Yes, of course."

"Thank you again. Please tell the others I'll be down again directly," she said brusquely. "I need to change my dress."

While she was speaking to him, she was looking past him to the card table. Lawrence had the distinct feeling that she thought him a blockish, dull fellow. While he was glad that she wasn't the sort of silly girl to bore him or bombard him with silly chatter, he felt a pang of injured pride. Perhaps his limp or his quietness put her off? But that was just as well, he told himself. If she was the sort of young lady who demanded an excess of flattery and a sparkling life, then the sooner that their families understood that he found her demands unacceptable, the better.

No doubt it was a good thing that Fortescue had come. It seemed very likely that a dashing blade like Fortescue was already succeeding as a fitting distraction.

When Eugenia returned to the noisy parlour a little while later, she had changed out of the periwinkle blue dress which had suited her so admirably, and was now wearing an older-looking, rose-coloured gown. Lawrence, who had begun to stand up in order to hold Eugenia's chair for her, was momentarily impeded by his injured leg, and Fortescue jumped up to perform this service in his stead.

As soon as Eugenia had taken her seat, she leaned forward and said, "Miss Lyle, I have put Mary to work on cleaning the spot." She proceeded to cast a quick glance at Lawrie as she settled back and took up her cards. He wondered if he was to blame for a ruined dress.

Marian said genially, "I am sure it will wash out nicely. We can be grateful that it was not a glass of wine or punch."

They played nearly an hour longer and Miss Lyle and Lawrence were soundly trounced by Miss Merritt and Fortescue.

In the spirit of exaggerated celebration, Fortescue rose from his seat and, with one hand behind his back, bowed over Eugenia's proffered hand. She laughed merrily as he led her from her seat and paraded her about, twirling her once in a circle and then returning her to her chair.

From across the room came a peal of uproarious laughter from the charade players quickly followed by a groan of feigned anguish.

The loud noises brought forth a barrage of barking from the dog. The little fellow ran to the middle of the room and made little rushes at the perpetrator of the perceived upset. Being told by Mr. Merritt in no uncertain terms to stop, Mister Cavendish sat down and howled.

Eugenia darted to the little dog, caught him up in her arms and soothed him, giggling appreciatively all the while. "We are fine, Mister Cavendish. Truly! Shush now. Stop your barking," and Mister Cavendish did.

It was time to say goodnight, and Hart brought the guests their evening coats and wraps.

The Trellaways were to take Miss Marian home before returning to their own. Everyone was packed tightly into the front hall, and Lawrie was helping Miss Lyle with her wrap. He turned abruptly to look for Fortescue and his right elbow made impact with a soft form behind him.

"You almost had me over!" It was Eugenia.

"I am so sorry, Miss Merritt," apologised Lawrie. "I- I am used to less refined company, it would seem!"

"The spill was my fault." She smiled contritely, "I was rushing about with a glass in hand. It was a careless action to be sure and my maid has me alone to thank for her evening laundry. Anyway, I am happy that you have come home from Spain without injury.... almost without injury, that is. For your parents' sake," she stammered.

Ah, she had noticed the limp. She coloured suddenly and looked down. Lawrie pressed his lips together and looked away.

"Oh, and thank you for bringing Captain Fortescue," she added.

He met her eyes briefly and nodded stiffly and said, "Of course, I am happy to please you, Miss Merritt."

John Fortescue, having heard his name on a lady's tongue, edged closer. He said goodnight warmly to all the Merritts, but most especially to Eugenia. Then, he took the arm of Miss Lyle, and they filed their way out the front door. There was nothing for it but for Lawrie to take up the rear with his walking stick in one hand and follow his family, friend and Miss Lyle out into the cool evening.

Chapter Three

"You know," commented Fortescue to Lawrie, one week and five days later as he was perusing the books in the study, "I don't find your Miss Merritt as undesirable as you do. She is neither homely nor silly. No," he added inhaling deeply, "in fact I've decided that she might be a bit of a country jewel!" He asked Lawrence to point him in the direction of the poetry books, and upon having the section pointed out to him, Fortescue lazily pulled down a thin volume that was resting along the top of others and, without reading the title, glanced back at Lawrie. "It must be that having grown up together you cannot see in her what I see. Or perhaps it is the ease of it? The knowledge that it was all settled for the two of you by your families."

Lawrence smiled a little and said blandly, "Perhaps it is as you say. It's the fixed-ness of it that revolts."

Although Lawrie secretly felt far less resolved to avoid the company of Miss Merritt than previously, he saw no reason to disclose his thoughts on the matter to his friend. Fortescue's stay was of an indeterminate duration, and while Lawrence had told himself that his friend would be doing him a service by distracting Eugenia, he couldn't help but find John's attraction to Miss Merritt an annoyance. Fortescue seemed intent on making up to Miss Merritt and putting more heart into it than Lawrence had expected.

Lawrie knew that his friend had no natural interest in literature, and right now he had hold of Charles Lamb's "Blank Verse", a volume very much full of thoughtful and sometimes humorous poetry but short on the sort of sensational romantic qualities that peppered the work of, say, Lord Byron. In short (thought Lawrie), while he himself admired it, he doubted that his friend would be long entertained.

Fortescue rapped a long finger on the worn, dark blue cover of the small book and smiled. "I think I may go out after tea. Do you care to join me? I believe Miss Merritt regularly takes a walk at this time. Perhaps we may meet!"

Lawrie declined the invitation. While he enjoyed country walks, limping in the company of Eugenia next to Fortescue did not appeal. The two of them could walk faster without him.

Instead, he would change his clothes and head out into the garden. He'd grown up following their old gardener about, and he still found peace out of doors amongst the trees and flowers.

"Go without me this time for I have some garden work that calls to me today. You'll not miss me."

"Ah, yes," said Fortescue, "I had forgotten that you go in for that sort of thing. Shovels and spades," he chuckled. "Right then, I shall see you afterwards."

"Very well. Enjoy your walk." With a nod and a tight smile, Lawrence took his leave to go upstairs for a change of clothes. A short time later he emerged from the house in an old pair of trousers and a loose shirt.

After a trip to the garden shed for tools and a short conversation with Davis, the old gardener, he was soon busy pruning damaged branches from the front hedge. It felt good to work again. His body, except for his left leg, missed the rigors of military life even if his mind did not. The country air, the birds and the solitude all felt good, and he began to whistle happily as he hacked and snipped.

Soon he was distracted by footfalls on the gravel path that ran from the house's front door to the gate at the road. Beyond the gate he heard the bark of a dog. Lawrie stood and shielded his eyes from the high sun and watched with interest as Fortescue hurried down the path and out the gate to meet Miss Merritt, her father and Eugenia's little dog as they passed.

Lawrie frowned, for there under John's elbow was his own treasured book.

Mere minutes before, Eugenia and her father had been enjoying a conversation on the topic of sheep breeding. Wonderful, ignorant Papa, thought Eugenia, what an oddity he allows me to be. I daresay I am quite a bluestocking and he has no notion of it.

When they neared the Trellaways' gate, Mister Cavendish began barking and Eugenia saw that Captain

Fortescue had emerged from the house. Her heart began to hammer when she saw that he was waving to her and appeared to be walking to meet them.

Her father went silent and said under his breath so that only Eugenia could hear, "The deuce!" and then cleared his throat loudly and said with false enthusiasm, "Well, well! Mr. Fortescue, impeccable timing. I don't suppose you'd care to join us for a stroll?" Giving the captain no time to reply he continued, "You've more important things to do, I daresay. A good day to you." With a nod, her father hurried forward.

"Actually, I would be delighted, sir," said Fortescue, darting forward and then falling into step beside Eugenia. At first, Mister Cavendish would have nothing to do with sharing his mistress, and he rushed the tall man, but Eugenia reprimanded the little dog and hauled him about to walk along the other side.

When she had got Cavendish under control she looked up and, just for an instant, she caught sight of Lawrence in the garden well beyond the gate. He was quite shocking! His hair was mussed, his shirt unbuttoned at the collar and his sleeves rolled up. He was holding a handful of bush trimmings. Was he scowling? Eugenia felt an almost irresistible urge to wave, more to provoke Lawrie than anything. Why should he be so serious and disagreeable?

She felt as awkward as he obviously did about their parents' cherished expectations, but that was no reason to behave rudely. One of them would offer or be offered for by someone else acceptable and that would be that. Or, with any luck, she might convince her parents to let her stay unmarried. She wasn't at all convinced that a husband was worth losing her independence for. Most men would not appreciate her active interest in running estate and farm operations. She'd learned to suppress her knowledge of livestock and plants when in public as she'd learned that her education and participation in such conversations was generally frowned upon. Living with a husband, she'd decided, must be like holding one's breath overlong, unable to be oneself. How deplorable! Some husbands and wives publicly ridiculed and shamed one another for such quirks in personality. And as for breeding, any girlish, prudish notions she might have had about that were squelched by years spent in barns and fields with her father and the farm help.

She looked away from the glowering Lawrence and focused on making Captain Fortescue comfortable. She and her father asked polite questions about the war and learned from his responses that he had been heavily involved in direct action as had Trellaway.

"Though I was made a captain through the untimely death of my predecessor, I would not have distinguished myself so very much, nor have saved so many lives of our men, had it not been for the tireless help I received from Trellaway."

Eugenia looked up at John with sudden interest, "What do you mean? How did you distinguish yourselves, you and Mr. Trellaway?"

"You ought to ask Trellaway himself to tell you more. He was made lieutenant, you know. I shouldn't like to say more than is fit for a young lady's ears, but I believe it is perfectly acceptable to say that, whilst I did what I could to draw enemy fire and keep the troops in order, Trellaway discreetly dispatched messages, pulled injured men from the field and transported them to medical stations." He paused and sighed. "Ever in the background but faithful to the last. I've never witnessed such quiet bravery. He was shot in the leg and the wound turned nasty. 'Lucky you didn't lose it altogether', he was told. It happened while running a message to the hospital tent."

Eugenia's father nodded his head vigorously. "Sounds like young Lawrence. Always in the background, giving others the centre stage."

Eugenia looked apologetically at Fortescue and attempted reparation for her father's rather pointed comment by saying loudly, "I'm sure we shouldn't consider bravery in war the same as attention-seeking for one's own vanity, Papa." And then to Fortescue she added softly, "Pray excuse us."

When they had walked their fill and were back in front of the Trellaways', Fortescue pulled a worn book from under his arm, and held it out to Eugenia. Receiving the volume into her gloved hand, she looked up at him in surprise. He had not struck her as a reading man, but rather a man of sport. Perhaps she had misjudged him? She looked down at the book, turning it in her hand so that she could read the cover.

"*Blank Verse by Charles Lamb*" she read aloud.

"Have you read it already?" asked Fortescue.

"No, I haven't. It sounds very far from 'The Mysteries of Udolpho'," she smiled.

"Is that a compliment to my taste or an insult?" teased Fortescue.

"I intended it as a compliment, sir," replied Eugenia with a laugh.

Fortescue gave her a last, exceedingly handsome grin and bowed his head to her first, then to her father, then lifted his hat, opened the gate, and took his leave.

Eugenia looked around curiously to see if Lawrie was still about, but she did not see him.

To her surprise, when Fortescue had gone, all her father said was, "What volume of silly love poems did the soldier give you to read?"

"They are not silly love poems. At least I do not think they are, judging by the title. It's a volume called, "Blank Verse" by Mr. Charles Lamb."

"Lamb? Yes," here Mr. Merritt harrumphed and then went on more brightly. "Before we were interrupted by the soldier--"

"Captain. He is a captain. We must be respectful."

"The name Lamb reminds me that, before being in-terrupted by the captain, we were talking about sheep, lambing season, were we not?"

"Yes, we were, Papa" she chuckled, affectionately taking his arm.

They meandered home deep in conversation with Mister Cavendish sniffing and trotting next to his mistress.

Chapter Four

After so many days of clear skies, the rain was bound to return. Oh, the day had begun fairly enough, but as Lawrence made his way as quickly as he could through the centre of the village, he thought it best to open his umbrella as the drops which were beginning to fall were the size of peas.

By the time he was at the end of the last block, the rain was pouring down! He jumped inside Pimm's, the fancy grocery, to stay dry and make a purchase more out of guilt for taking shelter than necessity. He decided upon some coffee berries, a taste for which he'd picked up on the continent. As he approached the counter, his attention was diverted by a figure outside. Through the window he saw a lady hunched over a large basket dart up and press herself against the glass in an attempt to take shelter under the narrow eaves of the shop. Lawrie quickly made his purchase and hurried to assist the young woman. Her bonnet was floppy and creased. Rivulets of water were dripping off the front of it and her dress was already starting to cling to her figure most improperly. Idiot girl. There didn't appear to be anyone with her and she must have forgotten her umbrella.

Mindful of the shopkeeper's suspicious stare, he opened the front door, put up his umbrella and turned to offer his assistance.

"Miss? May I..." he stopped and then finished incredulously, "Miss Merritt?"

Eugenia blinked up at him, water trickling down her face. She stiffened before replying through clenched teeth, "Hello, Mr. Trellaway."

Lawrie studied her critically, "What are you doing out without an escort? Not even your dog, and apparently, not even an umbrella!? I can only imagine your parents will agree that this was very thoughtless, even for you."

He pressed himself against the glass next to her.

"Thoughtless? Even for me?" Eugenia's eyes flashed angrily.

"I apologise for saying it, but I daresay I am correct. Here, allow me walk you home."

Eugenia stood up as straight as she could with the basket pressed into her waist. She appeared as though she were on the verge of giving him a set down when Lawrie chuckled. He couldn't help himself.

Turning to face the street, Lawrence held the umbrella more over the lady than himself and said, "I would offer you my arm properly, but you see I need to hold the umbrella with one hand and my walking stick with the other. Here," he nudged her gently with his elbow. "I do not know what it is that you carry in your basket, but your lovely bonnet is getting ruined."

"You're right." Eugenia looked at him out of the corner of her eye and her expression softened. She took his arm and said, "Thank you, Mr. Trellaway. And what's more, I admit that it was foolish of me to walk out without my umbrella. Father is at his solicitor's office just there," and she pointed past Lawrie's left shoulder. "He will be angry with himself when he realises that it is raining. I'm sure he is poring over papers and has no idea the sort of pouring that I am under out of doors. Anyway," she shrugged, "I was on my way with this basket to the Pratchetts'. If it is alright with you, I will borrow your shelter just as far as their home."

"Of course," answered Lawrence. He found that now that the commonplace was out of the way, he felt rather tongue-tied in Eugenia's company. This state, however, could not last long with her.

She sighed noisily and said, "I expect you're wondering what I am doing at the Pratchetts'?"

Lawrie gasped, "I would never be so ungentlemanly as to wonder."

"That's a very proper response, although I doubt it's true," she chortled. "Still, I shall tell you. I have been treating their milk cow who nearly died of infection."

"A milk cow?"

"Go ahead and laugh. I am prepared for it."

Lawrie smiled but he did not laugh.

Eugenia stopped abruptly and faced him. "Go ahead! Say it!"

He stopped and looked down at her curiously. "Say what, Miss Merritt?"

"How ridiculous I am."

"I don't think you are ridiculous. No. There are not many women that can cure livestock and many men of experience will refuse to do so for a family that cannot pay. Unless something has changed, the Pratchetts are beneath the notice of livestock professionals."

"More so than before," said Eugenia, biting her lower lip. "Mrs. Pratchett is now a widow and that is their only cow."

"Well then," said Lawrie in a low voice, "that makes you positively angelic."

"Oh, hardly. I'm afraid it's only an excuse for mucking about with cows."

"The child you used to be always had an orphaned or lame animal about" said Lawrie with a little smile playing about his lips. "I seem to remember an incident with chicks, as well as numerous lambs and puppies, even a hedgehog and a fox. Are you reduced to a single dog now?"

"Nearly. I do have a young rabbit with an injured leg." They stepped around a mud puddle together and then she went on. "Like you, I am learning how to take care of the estate, so in a way I have more pets than ever before, but now they sleep in the fields and cowsheds."

"I have the distinct impression that your parents desire you to marry."

A brief silence followed this comment, and Lawrie wished he had not broached the subject so early in their reacquaintance.

"Marry you, yes. But I will not, have no fear." She held up a gloved hand in a gesture of humble apology without looking at his face whilst she spoke. "I am completely, almost absolutely certain that I'm not fit for marriage," confided Eugenia, "which is why I am discreetly learning all I can from my father. He cannot help but treat me like a son, you know. I tell you in confidence that it's terribly simple to get him to show me how to do accounts and plan for the herds and haying, for he is very susceptible to flattery."

"Well," began Lawrie, choosing his words carefully. "What if someone entirely suitable were to offer for you and you were to convince your parents that he would make you happy?"

Eugenia replied confidently, "The question might then be, would I make him happy? For although I do not believe myself to be a difficult female, I do know that I might be considered a managing sort. Not that I think I would browbeat a husband that was at least as reasonable as my-self." They made their way around a large pit in the road, now filled with water before she continued. "No," she shook her head. "I do not think I would. But I am used to running a farm and household, and I am not so green as to suspect that with most men that might not sit well. So, you see, you are free to seek another if your parents will grant you their blessing to do so." Neither of them spoke for several moments, and Eugenia didn't see the shadow that had crossed Lawrie's face. "We're just coming upon the Pratchetts'. Please forget I said anything silly, won't you? But do remember this: if you intend to stay in your family home then we shall see each other very often, and I want you to know that we are childhood friends, but that is all."

Lawrence looked at her, his mouth slightly open, and Eugenia blinked up at him and waited a moment for a response but he could think of nothing to say.

Eugenia was distracted by someone at the Pratchetts' and she turned away to wave. To Lawrie she said, "Well, thank you again, Lawr- Mr. Trellaway. My father will call for me here on his way home. You needn't wait."

"You are welcome, of course, Miss Merritt. I hope to enjoy your company again on a drier day." He was rewarded with a cheerful glance and an open smile as she settled the basket again on her hip. Before she could hurry off, Lawrie took her wet, gloved hand and wrapped it around the umbrella handle. Quickly, he stepped out from beneath its shelter and with a final nod, pulled his cap down tightly and trudged off in the direction of home. He turned to watch surreptitiously from a little distance as she rushed in through the broken-down gate and was let into the house.

Lawrence was grateful to be without an umbrella in the falling rain, he decided, for it gave him an excuse to look down, ostensibly to avoid puddles and keep the raindrops from stinging his eyes. It was time that he paid attention to where he was going, both literally and metaphorically. He had to admit that, rather than reinforcing his disdain for settling for a childhood playmate who ought to have irritated him, the more he conversed with the woman Eugenia, the more he was impressed by her.

He enjoyed her free way of speaking. After seeing so much of the world, he did not think he could adjust to the restraints of common speech, those untruths that passed for politeness. It was his opinion that England could not continue in the old way. There were changes ahead for all of them, and how could one confront the future without honest conversation? He liked the way Eugenia lit up when she talked about country life. He would prefer a wife that had opinions and an education on such things as gardens and livestock, or anything, really. He was not the sort of man to be threatened by knowledge however it came, by man, woman or life experience.

Lawrence hit his boot upon a stone, nearly losing his footing, and emitted an oath. A pain shot up his leg and he had to pause and knead the muscle with his hand for a moment, but the discomfort soon subsided, and he moved forward into the driving rain. Could his leg be partly to blame for Eugenia's willingness to release him?

It was obvious from her words that she in no way considered him a suitor, and he ought to have been grateful that she was trying to make her wishes known in the kindest way she could; and she'd implied that as friends from childhood, their familiarity, their family connections, made them too well-acquainted to be attractive to one another.

He had been aware of the pleasure of her touch on his arm, with her body pressed against his side as they walked. The memory of it made him mutter, "Well, dash it... she may feel that way about me, but I, most definitely, do not feel that way about her." With these thoughts for company, he continued home.

Not many days after, Fortescue was taken ill. Nothing terrible, but chills and a cold were bad enough to land him in bed.

The mistress of Trellaway House, and Mrs. Perry, the cook, plied their guest with tisane and toast while the captain kept to his room.

Lawrence came to ask after Fortescue's health only to be shooed away in a friendly way.

"I'll be up and around in a snap!" said John. "I don't care to have you up here to be sneezed upon. Go tend your garden, Trellaway, if that rain has stopped." Fortescue tapped his fingers on his breakfast tray restlessly. "Now that I think about it, why don't you bring me something to read? I was never much of a reader, but I think now would be as good a time as any to begin, oh, and..." He said, grinning at Lawrie, "I loaned one of your books to our enchanting Miss Merritt. I should have asked first."

Lawrence retorted with a dismissive wave of his hand. "It doesn't signify. I hope she enjoys it." He couldn't resist a chuckle, however, and he added, "Only, if you knew the Merritts as I do, you'd have known that a manual on the cultivation of beans or a guide to a better calving season might have entertained just as well. Like most of us here, the Merritts are gentrified farmers." Here Lawrie paused for emphasis, "Even Miss Merritt always has a bit of straw upon her hem or a hen under her arm.

"Anyway," said Lawrie, as he rose to leave, "do rest, old fellow. I will be back momentarily with a sporting book for you. And what's more, I swear I will do nothing of interest while you are laid up, but instead will apply my fullest efforts to the spreading of mulch."

"Mary?" called Eugenia, "it is time for our walk!" Eugenia paused at her front door, drawing on her gloves, as Mister Cavendish came skidding around the corner, his leash in his mouth. "You are ready then, aren't you?" she laughed, fondly ruffling up his fur as she attached his lead. As she straightened up, she espied the blue-bound book that Captain Fortescue had loaned her last week.

There was no denying she had enjoyed it. In fact, she'd read it cover to cover rather quickly, and decided that farm journals were not the only interesting reading after all. Though she'd not considered herself a romantic girl, she found that poetry affected her deeply and she was rather surprised that Captain Fortescue would have such an interest in lyrical observations of the natural world. It made him that much more charming. In fact, he was exactly the sort of man with whom she used to imagine falling in love.

She picked up the book and carefully slid it into her reticule. There was nothing untoward in returning the book, was there? It was likely that she would not see the captain, but old Dobson, their butler, or one of the young Trellaways. Finally, Mary joined her at the door and the two of them, with Mister Cavendish, sallied forth.

As the Trellaways' home came into view, Eugenia could not help the pounding of her heart. "Mary, please let us stop for just a moment to return a book."

Eugenia stepped off the road to enter through the gate and fished around inside her bag for the book. Then, out of the corner of her eye, she saw Mary curtsy. Someone was approaching from the house. Eugenia looked up quickly, only to find that it was not Captain Fortescue after all, but Lawrie.

He was dressed in his work clothes again and as he approached her, he removed his work gloves and inclined his head politely to each of the women. "Hello Miss Merritt, Mary. May I assist you in some way?" he asked as he opened the gate to them, and Eugenia stepped inside.

Unwilling to appear forward, Eugenia hesitated and blushed furiously. She was not sure how to proceed and she quickly cast around in her mind for some other reason to be here.

Lawrie said hastily, "Ah, please excuse my appearance. You have caught me mulching the flower beds in the side yard." He gave her a cautious smile. "My apologies."

Coming to her wits, Eugenia said, "Oh no! No need to apologise! I fancy that you must enjoy a good afternoon spent in the garden with weather as fine as it is today. I certainly do." She lowered her eyes and bit her lip. Lawrie looked exceedingly handsome in his work clothes, with his collar open and shirtsleeves rolled up. "Is... is your guest at home?" she forced herself to ask. After all, it was the captain she was supposed to be talking to.

Lawrie's smile grew smaller and became a bit fixed. "Fortescue? Yes, he is here but he has taken ill. Nothing serious I should say, but he is in his room today, reading. Do not worry."

Eugenia's eyes opened wide, and she fluttered prettily. "Oh no, I shan't worry. He seems quite a fit fellow and I only just learned that he has excellent taste in reading. I was rather surprised, actually." Here she blushed a deeper shade of pink. "In fact, I have a book to return to him." She held out the volume to Lawrie, who moved closer to her, exciting the attention of Mister Cavendish. The little dog whined and jumped up on Lawrie's legs, earning him a sharp reprimand from his mistress. Lawrence didn't appear to be in the least offended by Mister Cavendish's rude behavior because he bent down to scratch the little dog just behind the ears.

"He's not a beauty, but he's fiercely loyal," she volunteered.

"So I see," said Lawrie, standing again, "and you know how to value it."

There was something shining in his blue eyes, some light she had not noticed before. Was he, or was he not, the boy she had known in childhood?

With a quick recovery and smile, Eugenia pushed the book at Lawrence who reached out and took it.

"Please thank the captain for me. He loaned me his book and I very much enjoyed it."

To her surprise, Lawrence seemed to find this inordinately funny, for he laughed suddenly. It made his eyes crinkle at the corners, and he seemed transformed some-how. She thought he should laugh more often.

He pocketed the small volume, and said, "I will thank him for his thoughtfulness in loaning you one of my books, yes."

"Oh dear!" was all that Eugenia could think to say at first, but the humour of the situation struck her, and her eyes brightened, and she laughed, then she made a move-ment to leave when, from behind her, Lawrie blurted out, "How did you enjoy it, then?"

Eugenia turned around to answer him, but she decided that it was easier to think clearly when she did not look directly into his eyes but focused instead on his forehead. "It was diverting to be sure. It reminded me that, while Papa and I share a passion for agricultural journals, there is something to be enjoyed in a book of poetry. I have never thought of the world in just such a way, you see. I'm afraid my conscious thoughts and even appreciation for nature have tended toward the prosaic, but truly I think the comfort I find in my flower beds, or a fine sunset, is more than that and now I have more words to feel with." She paused for a moment. "Words can be like spices and spring herbs after a winter of leeks and plain pies, can they not?"

Lawrence smiled at this. "Just so," he agreed. "I think that is an apt analogy."

"The captain joined my father and I on our walk the other day. That is when he loaned me your book."

Eugenia saw Lawrie look away, but she rushed on with-out knowing why she felt driven to tell him how she felt about what she had learned about him from the captain's stories. "He told us how brave you were there - in the war, I mean. Not only boldly facing combat but concealing and comforting fallen men or getting them to the medical tents. That's how you were injured, he told us. And not only that, but you had done so numerous times, fully knowing what you risked."

He was silent for a moment, and looked away, frowning. "That was not the difficult part," he said. "Hiding and protecting was easy. It was the rushing and killing for which one cannot forgive oneself, nor so easily forget." Lawrie's brows furrowed and his mouth curled so unpleasantly that Eugenia comprehended that she had led him to unpleasant thoughts, a wake of painful memories. She tried to steer the conversation to calmer waters.

"And you are home now to recreate?"

"I am home to work. My father wants me to take over his duties, and I feel it will add to my happiness to do so."

"The quiet country life, then? I should think it difficult to return after having been to cities and having chased Spanish forces hither and --" but here she stopped, realising that she had circled back to the war.

"I should have thought you'd understand, Miss Merritt," Lawrie answered with an appraising look. "And then there's the matter of the leg."

Eugenia found herself at a loss to know how to respond, but at this moment Mary cleared her throat, just audibly enough to remind her mistress of propriety, and Eugenia knew that she was delaying longer than appropriate.

"Please tell Captain Fortescue that I, and my family," she added hastily, "hope that he soon will find his health restored. Good day, Mr. Trellaway."

Lawrence bowed slightly and said, "Goodbye, Miss Merritt, and my best to your parents."

Eugenia nodded in assent and Lawrie ushered her through the gate.

Lawrence watched the ladies start off on their way, jerked on his gloves, and returned to his shovelling, this time a bit savagely. He did not at all feel like passing Eugenia's well-wishes for a hasty recovery along to the ailing Fortescue. No - not by a long shot, he didn't.

Chapter Five

Eugenia sat in the window seat, stroking the rabbit with the broken leg. She looked thoughtfully at the small round table next to her that held a magnificent bouquet of flowers. Her mother swept into the room and glared at the arrangement.

"They're just flowers, Mama."

Her mother harrumphed and walked out again.

Captain Fortescue had brought her the flowers yesterday along with a second book of poetry. This time he had not borrowed one from the Trellaways' shelves but had gone to town to buy her a copy of her own to keep. She knew he had because he had told her so and had written her name in the front of it, signing his own name beneath hers. She had looked long and hard at their names. What would it be like to be Mrs. Captain John Fortescue? She sighed a little and frowned.

When the captain had come with the flowers and the book, he had been shown out to the garden. Eugenia had been wearing her huge straw bonnet and dirty apron over an ancient day dress which, though once a lively green, had faded to an indeterminate shade of yellowish grey, and boots. She had looked up when she heard him coming through the garden gate and fished a stray strand of hair from her eyes as she squinted up at him. He had laughed when he had seen her, and she felt herself blush.

"No need to work for your blossoms! I have brought you some here."

He had smiled kindly and tilted his handsome head. "I left Trellaway in his garden just minutes ago. Said he'd got some seeds to plant instead of joining me down here. Pleasure in sport, I understand; shooting, riding, racing, even fishing... but plant cultivating? That requires far too much patience for men of my stamp."

He paused, as if he suddenly recalled something, and said, "Hello, wait a moment," and began rummaging in his blue jacket pocket. He grinned and pulled out a grubby grey rag, wadded into a messy ball and handed it to her. "For you from Trellaway. A fruit of his labours."

Eugenia bent her head and slowly unwrapped several small bulbs. She looked up questioningly.

"Dahlias, he says. White ones."

Eugenia smiled, "Do please thank him for me, won't you? But one thing bothers me; by your admission, do you say that Mr. Trellaway is not a man such as yourself?"

"Trellaway? Oh, he is the best of men, the very best. I told you of how he risked his life more than once to save the lives of our fellows, always discreetly as is his way, but as he admits, and I take nothing from him by repeating, while the occasional adventure is good, his heart is at its core that of a country squire and not a sporting man."

"Is that so?"

"I must have diversions and challenges beyond what can be found in country life. Have you never been to London, Miss Merritt?"

Eugenia shook her head. "I confess I have not." She returned her gaze to her plants, moving forward with her cutters. She made a couple of snips, then mused aloud, "When one is used to such places, I can imagine a retiring life might be rather a trial. Do you know where you are off to next?"

She looked up at him and he smiled into the sky, hands loose in his pockets. "I am awaiting my next commission, but as an officer I shall have some say in the matter. Or-" he paused, "if someone dear to me were to have a preference." Without waiting for a reaction or acknowledging that he had spoken so boldly, he crossed his arms and strolled to the rabbit hutch next to the back door and bent to peer inside.

"Dinner?" he asked with a smirk, looking over at Eugenia.

He looked so frightfully handsome, the sort of carefree, tall and confident man that Eugenia had always thought she'd swoon over (if one were ever to venture into the little hamlet of Cherrybrook), that she could almost forgive him for suggesting the little rabbit was to be eaten like any ordinary rabbit. Almost, but not quite.

She felt her smile become a bit more fixed. Her heart was no longer in it. Eugenia answered his questions simply, for her mind was in a turmoil. In fact, she fancied that she was content when the captain bid her good day and took his leave.

As time went on, it seemed to Eugenia that Captain Fortescue had to spend half his days waiting for her to pass by the Trellaways' on her walks, because without fail he was ready to join her and whoever was her chaperone. Eugenia looked for Lawrie, too. She couldn't help wishing he would accompany his friend some of the time, and she thought it odd that Lawrie never joined the small walking party. There were a few occasions when she did catch sight of him, but he was in the doorway of the house or out in the garden, and like a figure in a clockwork, he would wave to her and then retreat.

One day when Captain Fortescue came whistling from the side garden, he brought with him a brown paper packet of seeds.

"Sweet peas here. A most enchanting colour, according to Trellaway. Peachy coloured and they smell just as sweet. Plant them next Good Friday for added luck. For you with his regards, he says."

Eugenia smiled broadly and casually looked about for Lawrie, but he did not appear.

Eugenia's parents secretly feared the handsome threat to their fond hopes.

Mrs. Merritt was in favour of a good long talk with their daughter to try to bring her to reason, but Mr. Merritt looked at her darkly over the rims of his spectacles and said, "Remember the chickens, Lettie?" And that was all he needed to say. Eugenia was stubborn, and the best way for her to come to her senses, he was convinced, was for her to find her own way.

Once, when Eugenia was young, she had insisted upon hatching a brood of chickens by moving a half dozen eggs about the house trying to keep them warm, turning them and carrying them about with her. They were all she talked about from sunup to sundown.

She successfully nurtured three eggs and these chicks pecked their way into the welcoming world of Eugenia's bedroom.

She was so pleased that she cried. Her mother patted her daughter's back thoughtfully and wondered if the mothering of chicks wasn't just a bit too taxing on such a young girl.

Nothing would do but for Eugenia to keep the chicks in a box in her room. They grew quickly and Mrs. Merritt told her daughter that this had gone on quite long enough and would she please put them in the henhouse where they belonged. The young Eugenia's face fell and then she got a look in her eyes, and she stuck out her chin defiantly and said that she could handle them quite well and it would break her heart to let them in with "that lot."

In exasperation, Mrs. Merritt had gone raving to Mr. Merritt and would he "please come and talk to the girl and make her see good sense?" But instead, Mr. Merritt told his good wife that, with Eugenia's passionate nature and strong will to nurture everything from seedlings to sick sheep, it may be best to let her learn by experience why every family does not live with chickens in their home.

"Let her burn out her desire, my love," he had said. "She's a sensible girl, if overly dramatic at times, but she'll come to right thinking and will learn from the doing of it rather than our censorship."

Mr. Merritt's prediction had proven correct. Not one more week of carrying and coddling and talking nonstop about the poor little creatures passed before the smell, the noise, and the around the clock responsibility grew to be too much for Eugenia.

She put the pullets in the henhouse, cleaned her room of the chicken nursing station, slept late the next morning and there was not another word spoken.

Chapter Six

"**R**eally, Mother?! A dance? Me?"

Lawrence, usually so mild, burst out at this pronouncement and ran his hand in frustration through his hair. Then he let his hand fall, slapping the table in front of him. He looked away for a moment and rose stiffly. "I am sorry, Mother. I ought to be grateful," he said quietly. With a nod, he left the room.

Mrs. Trellaway sighed. She knew such an event would not show Lawrence to an advantage, but he could not stay home when the ball was Cherrybrook's expression of delight for the safe return of the soldiers and officers. He was to be an honoured guest.

Doubtlessly the captain would be the central attraction for all the eligible ladies, including Eugenia. The captain was such a likeable young man but the good lady acknowledged to herself that right now she wished him at Jericho.

The marked attention that Fortescue was paying to Eugenia had caused Mrs. Trellaway to take to her bed with headaches more than once already, and as Lawrie had just left in a sour mood, she felt another megrim coming on.

She rubbed the back of her neck absent-mindedly and called for the tea dishes to be taken to the kitchen.

That afternoon from her bedside, she entreated her husband to speak with Lawrence.

"My dear, you must do something! To be forced to lie here and watch as the captain sweeps away with Lawrie's Eugenia....".

"Well, if you are in bed, you cannot be watching too closely, can you?" Mr. Trellaway observed grimly. He walked to the window and looked out at the falling rain. With a small sigh, he added, "If there is no way to stop their attachment, you may be assured that Lawrie knows right from wrong and will put it to his friend that he ought to offer for her. We are not to interfere."

His pronouncement did nothing to comfort his wife, whose answer was to moan and cover her eyes. Mr. Trellaway grimaced and left off looking out the window. He sat on the edge of her bed and took her hand, patting it tenderly. After a moment, Mrs. Trellaway opened one eye and said, "I suppose you are right. We cannot drive him off. And, after all, he did so much for Lawrie in Spain... but promise me that you will intervene should the neighbours begin to talk of it."

Mr. Trellaway agreed and took out his spectacles from his breast pocket. Putting them on, he said, "Ah! Now let me see you dry your eyes." He smiled indulgently at her. "There she is, my beautiful wife. Now, you have a little rest and I'm certain that you will soon feel better."

The afternoon before the dance, Eugenia was sitting at her dressing table staring straight ahead at her looking glass. She was looking very hard, as if trying to understand herself from the outside.

Captain Fortescue had been most attentive for the past few weeks, and at the first mention of the upcoming dance, he had appeared on their doorstep with a nosegay and the request to be the first to dance with Eugenia.

There had never been a young man in Cherrybrook to interest her, and it had been easy to pretend that life would always go on as it did now, but she knew (or finally admitted to herself) that it wouldn't. She did not want to be a spinster. Not really. She loved her parents, but they would one day be infirm, and it was foolish to pretend her father and mother would always be able to care for her. No, someday it would be her turn to care for them.

Besides, she wanted a brood of children to mother, and she'd need a husband to get them by.

She saw that her reflection didn't even blush at the thought.

These conditions being as they were, she ought to have been all of a fluster over a likely offer of marriage from the captain. No gentleman would fail to speak after so much obvious attention. She felt no heightened emotion. Oh, she felt nervous, yes, but not happy. She should be happy.

Captain John Fortescue was the right sort of dashing – the kind a lady could boast of catching, yet not such a coxcomb that you feared he'd not keep his vows or turn out to be an unworthy father or poor provider.

Fortescue was friendly, he liked flowers. He did not seem to care much about growing them, but he knew she liked them.

He liked books. Well, he hadn't read much. He had been "too busy hunting and then off like a shot to the military," he'd said. But he knew that she liked reading.

He liked the country. On occasion.

He liked sports, if not the sort of ambling about and exploring she enjoyed.

She would probably have to leave Cherrybrook. Here she saw her reflected frown deepen. She'd become an army wife, either left at his family home for months while he was away, or she would be following him from town to town. While the prospect excited her curiosity, because she did so want to travel a little, it also meant that she couldn't cultivate her own gardens and have one cosy home to return to for all the years ahead. Besides, who would care for Mister Cavendish and look after her parents?

Eugenia decided that she simply must feel needed, necessary to the man she was to marry. She had little patience with useless things and she herself certainly did not want to become one.

Why hadn't her parents openly objected to Fortescue? Forbade her to see him? They would have to have been ignorant indeed not to see how he favoured her. They had to know. And what about their blasted plan for her to marry Lawrie? How could they give up so easily?

But then she considered that her parents, her father especially, seldom refused her what she wanted unless they thought it truly harmful. Also, the captain was a guest of the Trellaways. They would not wish to create a breach in such an old friendship unless something inappropriate were to happen.

Would her father allow her to marry Captain Fortescue? Did he believe that Lawrie was no longer likely to ask for her?

Lawrie. She dropped her gaze to the packet of sweet peas he had sent her by way of Fortescue. Before, seeing the small packet of seeds resting there had cheered her, but this time when she noticed it, she felt angry instead. Why was Lawrie stepping aside so easily? Was she so undesirable that he was content to let the captain court her under his very nose? Before his own front gate? Was he that pleased to accept her offer of friendship alone, never to think of her as more than an old friend and neighbour?

There was the frightfully wet day when he had found her in town without an umbrella or escort. Even though she was at first embarrassed, she enjoyed the brief walk on his arm and their honest conversation. She was aware that she could be exactly who she was with Lawrie. He didn't scold her or try to diminish her passion for field and flower, or even her concern for doctoring sick and injured beasts. He was thoughtful and kind. He himself shared her love for growing things and affection for their country life.

Next, she recalled when Lawrie had met her at his front gate when she stopped to return the book. He had smiled a lot and laughed. She'd never felt so keenly aware of a man before. She remembered just how he had appeared, sweaty and sunned, his sleeves rolled up and his collar open. She had noticed the fair hair on his forearms and the well-toned muscles. She noticed how his thighs showed strong through his trousers when he'd bent down to pet Mister Cavendish. She had felt a sudden and peculiar sort of dizzy, hot sensation that day she had never felt before. Why, she even remembered liking how Lawrie smelled! He smelled pleasantly of perspiration and some sort of spice mixed with fresh soil.

Her mirrored reflection was most certainly flushed.

How could Fortescue be so winsome, and yet so unaffecting? The captain was simply a face to her, though an attractive face.

Lawrie was a whole man. Oh, she liked his face, yes, his cornflower blue eyes, thoughtful, slow blinks, and small, straight mouth. But something about him felt more than the sum of his parts. Heavens, it was good Mama wasn't able to hear her thoughts! There was some hitherto unknown quality that drew her to him, and, he felt like home. He belonged where she belonged.

Eugenia stared at herself, her lips open just a little, and she gasped. It seemed likely that she was feeling the first stirrings of love. She laid her hand gently over her heart. Was she attracted to Lawrie? But what must he think of her?

Chapter Seven

L ike roosters and hens.

This was the sight that met Eugenia's eyes when she first entered the small upstairs ballroom on the arm of her father. All around were women in feathered headdresses nodding their plumed heads and fluttering fans. Bearded men with tall, combed hair and tailcoats pecked at food from small plates. Eugenia nearly laughed to think how much like colourful garden fowl they all looked, herself included. Straightaway, her searching gaze found Marian against the wall, standing beside Marian's mother and younger siblings.

"Excuse me, Mamma. I will return directly. I see the Lyles just there and I'd like to greet them."

"Yes, my dear. You go ahead. Look how fine Marian looks tonight! She fairly glows! I suppose she made her gown. She has a talent to be sure." Mrs. Merritt smiled generously and turned back to follow her husband while Eugenia made her way to her friend's side.

"Marian, you look lovely! And thank goodness, no feathers."

"Whatever do you mean?" asked Marian with sincere wonder at her friend's comment as they clasped hands.

"Chickens, Marian."

Marian's eyebrows shot up and she looked around the room, then giggled. As she hugged Eugenia she said, "Oh, just look! I agree with you completely. Some of the fashions this season are ridiculous. Do you suppose that Mrs. Kent has an entire pheasant on her head?" Eugenia found Mrs. Kent almost immediately, for if there were a prize for the tallest headdress and the most feathers, that tiresome lady would be the winner. Biting her gloved knuckle to keep from laughing too loudly, Eugenia joined her friend in looking about the crowded ballroom. The musicians were tuning their instruments and more familiar faces were still entering through the double doors and meeting and mingling with friends.

"Look there! Do you see the couple just entering from the cloakroom, to the left of the door?" asked Marian, clutching Eugenia's arm. "That tall man is the new vicar at Wellsey, Mr. Morton. He has the hunter's green waistcoat and curly brown hair. I have met him because he has come to our house to consult with Papa. Mrs. Morton, his mother, is on his arm. They look very much alike, do they not? Both are elegant, yet there is something warm and sincere about them."

"Yes, they are. Those traits are most admirable in ministers and widows," agreed Eugenia. She whispered, "Observe, Marian, Mr. Morton has just set eyes on Miss Hamblin!" The two watched as Mr. Morton made his way steadily toward the receiving line and Miss Cherise Hamblin, the daughter of Lord and Lady Hamblin.

"And I cannot point," breathed Marian, "but look just to the left of the arches. There are the Trellaways and your captain."

"He is not my captain," said Eugenia firmly. "Why do you say that that?"

Marian ignored her question and went on. "There are about five more men in uniform. They all look terribly imposing in their regimentals." After a moment's pause, she continued. "I think I shall melt through the floor if any one of them should ask me to dance tonight."

Eugenia started to say that of course Marian would be asked to dance, and of course she would survive it, when she saw her mother summon her. She took leave from Marian, telling her friend that she had promised the first dance to Captain Fortescue and would talk to her again after the set was done. Hurrying as gracefully as she could through the little crowd, she caught up to her parents. Together, the Merritts shuffled along, weaving their way around their neighbours, sometimes stopping to talk or greet a friend. Slowly they made it to the head of the room and had just enough time to thank both Lord and Lady Hamblin, and greet Miss Hamblin before the musicians started up in earnest. The dancing would soon begin.

Recalling that Captain Fortescue would be looking for her, Eugenia spun on her heels and saw that she had already been discovered. Fortescue was wearing his finest smile and was making his way towards her. Behind him, against the wall near his parents, stood Lawrence. He looked very fine in his uniform she thought, but his arms were crossed over his chest, and his expression was impenetrable. For a moment, their gazes locked - but then Fortescue was before her, bowing, and blocking Lawrie from view.

Eugenia struggled to fix what she hoped was a pleasant and inviting look of tranquil pleasure as she bent neatly in a curtsy, happy for the chance to look down at the floor before looking up into the eyes of Captain John Fortescue. She thought that she had never seen such an earnest look of admiration in his eyes before, and as he guided her safely into position on the dance floor, she bit her lip in agitation. Having placed her in the line of ladies near the centre of the room, he stepped across from her and took his place between two middle-aged gentlemen. Eugenia forced herself to meet his eyes. Her heart began to race. She told herself that she was being a goose. Was there really anything different in his look tonight? She glanced back at Lawrie but he was in conversation with his father and hers. The musical introduction ceased, she gulped, and the dancing began.

Never had she been so glad of gloves! Her palms were sweating profusely and it would have been such a humiliation for anyone to know, especially Captain Fortescue. Being the first dance of the evening, while all the ladies were feeling their freshest, the dance was an easy one with steps that most of the attendees could be counted upon to remember. Thank goodness for that. If it had been a new dance, Eugenia might have found herself like a lost lamb in the middle of the room. Her feet and hands acted on instinct, taking her where she needed to be, circling, moving up the floor, down the floor, breaking away and coming together. Fortescue was an elegant dancer. Eugenia was happy to see Marian on the floor. She was a lovely girl, perhaps Fortescue – but no. He seemed to reserve a particularly heated look just for her. She tried to meet his intensity with a polite but sincere gaze, but her heart pounded so hard that the heat of the room made her head swim and she tripped. At the same time, she covered her mouth for fear she might be sick.

As she started to tumble to the floor, Fortescue grabbed her by the waist and one arm and pulled her up and out of the line of the other dancers, practically carrying her to the side of the room, setting her in a chair and bending down on one knee solicitously.

His face was lined with concern as he removed Eugenia's gloves and then he gripped one of her small hands tightly in his. "Why, you're experiencing chills, Miss Merritt. Your hands are damp. Your parents must fetch you home immediately!"

Her mother came bouncing into the small cluster of people crowded around her daughter in time to hear Fortescue's pronouncement.

Mr. Merritt pushed his way in and, taking Eugenia's hand in his, helped her stand and put his arm around her, waving off other offers of assistance, saying that he regretted their hasty departure, but anyone could see that the usually hale and hardy Eugenia wasn't feeling well.

As she was swept from the room, she was aware of overwhelming relief that Fortescue had not dropped to his knee to propose marriage, and she knew she had been cowardly enough to encourage the supposition that she was ill. Out of the corner of her eye, she saw Lawrie trying to make his way to her, but nearly a dozen chattering couples stood between them. She realised with dismay that her father and mother would have her down the narrow stairway and out to the waiting carriage before he would have time to weave his way through the crowded room.

When they arrived home, Eugenia allowed herself to be helped from the carriage and into the house. Mister Cavendish rushed this way and that about her feet, barking.

"Quiet, dog!" shouted her father. But Mister Cavendish trotted up the stairs and jumped onto Eugenia's bed in anticipation of his mistress. Her parents deposited her upon the edge of it and sent for Mary to help Eugenia undress while they fetched her a cup of tea.

In the flickering lantern light, Eugenia could see her silhouette in her mirror as she sat slumped on her bed, waiting for Mary. She looked at her reflection and shook her head slowly.

What a weakling! How could she have let the captain go so far without genuine discouragement? Now the whole town had seen him drop before her and hold her bare hand. What was worse, Lawrence would have seen the whole of it. If he hadn't, some eager gossip would have told him before her family carriage had left the park. She was sure of it.

She slouched even further, and a tear dropped on her wrist. She dug in her reticule for a handkerchief.

Mary knocked and entered her room.

"My goodness, miss! I didn't think anything was wrong with you when you went out. I am so sorry! To leave a dance, the captain, officers and all the soldiers dressed up in their regimentals receiving their medals? What a pity! But don't you worry, we will get you back in full health, quick as a wink."

"Thank you, Mary." Yes, I shall be well quite soon, thought Eugenia guiltily. Fear and humiliation heal quickly. For a moment she wondered if she ought to feign sickness until Fortescue grew bored with Cherrybrook and decided to leave.

Her dismal thoughts were interrupted by a second sharp rap on her door.

"Come in," she called out.

Her mother and father both stepped in.

"My dear, are you alright? Are you ill?" her mother asked.

Eugenia opened her mouth to answer, and nothing came out. She looked at Mamma and said in a small voice, "I do not know."

"You do not know? Was it a case of the nerves? We've never known you to be a delicate girl," her mother clasped her hands together, "but it is plain to see that we must prepare for an offer of marriage from Captain Fortescue."

Mrs. Merritt looked as unhappy as Eugenia felt, and Mr. Merritt pressed his fingers to his brows as if he were trying to drive an unpleasant thought into his head by force.

Even though Eugenia had no intention of accepting Captain Fortescue, it did not follow that he should be disdained by her parents. The captain had done nothing wrong. If anything, when they had begun their acquaintance, she had encouraged his attention and now was sorry for it, yet that was not his fault, but hers.

"You have nothing to say?" asked her father.

Eugenia looked up at him sadly. She didn't know how to comfort her beloved parent! Should she tell him that she would not accept an offer, or was he afraid that she would not, and miss her opportunity for a comfortable situation? Lawrence had done nothing to put himself forward when in the presence of her parents, and goodness only knew that if he had taken her words to heart that day in the rain, the only offer she would entertain from him would be one of friendship.

The mantel clock ticked infuriatingly loud.

Her father sighed. "Your mother and I will leave you to rest. Come, my dear," he said, and Mr. and Mrs. Merritt left the room.

Several hours later when the Trellaways and Captain Fortescue arrived home, all three of the men gathered for a last drink in the study. They were rather fatigued from their evening on display, and Lawrence had never been one for crowds. The elder Mr. Trellaway drained his glass and set it down on the side table, leaned forward with elbows out, and his hands on his thighs and said, "You boys were kept busy enough all night. I suppose you may be wondering as much as I how Miss Merritt has fared. I will call upon her in the morning and bring back a report, shall I?"

Both younger men started at once to protest, and Lawrence said, "No need. Fortescue and I will be happy to pay a visit to the Merritts early tomorrow and see how she is feeling."

Mr. Trellaway stood and nodded, sending a sharpish glance at his son, before bidding them goodnight.

Lawrence leaned back in the high-backed chair, relieved to be sitting down and once again in the blessed quiet of his family home. He crossed his arms behind his head, and looked up at the ceiling at nothing in particular.

Fortescue observed his friend for several silent minutes and took the rest of his brandy in a noisy swig before declaring abruptly, "I plan to leave here by the end of the week."

"What?" Lawrence started. "I confess I am shocked by your announcement. In fact, I cannot be pleased by it! " He sat up quickly. "What of Miss Merritt? I had rather thought that you of all men would understand that you have a duty now to that lady. I know better than to believe you a scoundrel and I see that to secure her would cause you no pain. You have been exceedingly attentive."

Fortescue laughed outright at this and said, "Trellaway, you amaze me! You have no need for me to offer for her when it is plain to see that you would not hesitate to do so yourself if I were not here."

Lawrence began to object, but John cut him off and held up his hand, "I believe that, despite your thoughtless projection about Miss Merritt when I had first arrived, you do have a tendre for her. Not only that, but after my last few calls upon the Merritts, I cannot think that she prefers me to you. Her unusual behavior at the dance this evening only confirmed my suspicion." Fortescue gave a low chuckle and put down his glass. "No," he said with conviction, "I am sure to meet with rejection from that quarter. It is time to say goodbye and bid you both happy. If I go quickly and pain you little, may I expect an invitation to your wedding?"

Lawrence stared at Fortescue. "You think you understand her feelings, then?"

"I assure you I do. Powers of practised observation, my friend," said Fortescue, tapping his temple. "I flatter myself that, at first, your Miss Merritt found me charming, but something I did or said along the way put her off." John cocked an eyebrow, "She looks for you, you know. When I call upon her or walk with her, she always casts about to see if you will join us. And tonight, when we danced, I had the distinct impression that I caused her genuine distress! When I assisted her to a chair it was as though she felt my hands were hot pokers, for she positively pitched herself out of them."

Lawrence thoughtfully settled back into the chair, crossed an ankle over a knee and ran his fingers through his hair until it stood untidily on end. He looked down at nothing in particular until a slow smile spread across his face. After a moment's reflection, he grinned broadly at Fortescue. Lawrence leant forward suddenly, snatched up his brandy glass and, with a nod to his friend, drained it. "You go ahead to bed, Fortescue. You must be spent and I find I suddenly have much to occupy my mind. I believe I need some time to reflect upon what you have said."

"Excellent decision," said John with a laugh. "Good-night, Trellaway."

Lawrence and John set out for the Merritt's home on horseback the following morning. It was a fine day, and as the birds sang and the stray breeze rustled the grassy fields that lined the narrow dirt road, Lawrence felt that nothing could disturb his sense of purpose and peace of mind.

"Look what you'll be missing if you leave now," he remarked jovially to Fortescue. "Think of all the fishing and good country sport of which you deprive yourself!"

Fortescue chuckled. "You'll be in Miss Merritt's pocket from here until goodness knows when. You'll scarcely realise I'm missing. Besides, you are always going on about your and Miss Merritt's belief in the benefits of an active life, 'straw on her hem', and all that. I hope you'll be able to manage her! I dare say she will keep you on your toes." Fortescue snorted with laughter, "I shall be sorry to miss bearing witness to it!"

Lawrence held up his hand with a smile. "I will hear no more now. You act as though it's as good as done. You were not present to hear her promise me undying friendship. She is a woman of the times. I can only hope that she believes that her habits and opinions must necessarily ostracise unfavourable suitors, and not that she actually wishes to remain unwed. Her parents cannot wish her to remain alone."

"Ah! And we finish with where we began... pleasing the parents."

When they rode into the Merritts' yard, they saw that Mr. Merritt had just seated himself in his gig and had taken up the lead lines. Seeing that he had visitors, Mr. Merritt waited until the younger men had dismounted, before urging his horse forward and pulling up short of them. Although he greeted them politely, he seemed unusually nervous. He licked his lips several times and kept looking back toward the house. In Lawrence's memory, he never recalled his father's friend as being anything but calm and cheerful.

"I suppose you are here to speak to my daughter?" inquired Mr. Merritt, with a grim smile.

"Yes, sir," said Lawrence. "We hope that she was not taken seriously ill?"

"No. no! Nothing wrong with that one. She seems to have recovered this morning. Always such a hale girl, but still, she was a bit peaked last night." Here he looked quickly at Fortescue, then averted his eyes. "I am just heading out as you see. I..." another pause. "I will not be in until this afternoon if you should have anything particular you wish to ask." Mr. Merritt's gaze darted almost desperately from Fortescue to Lawrence. Glancing heavenward, he took out his handkerchief from his front pocket and began to mop his brow.

It did not seem overly warm to Lawrence, who squinted up to survey the sky. In a flash, he heard the sound of crunching gravel as the gig suddenly shot forward, and he felt an excruciating pain in his left foot that caused him to cry out and crumple to the ground in anguish. He grabbed his lower leg in both hands and rolled over, shouting through gasps, "Damn and damn again!"

Fortescue stood momentarily rooted to the spot, his eyes bulging, and Lawrie heard Mr. Merritt jump out of the gig and hurry to where he lay.

Lawrie pinched his eyes tightly shut, but he heard a door being flung open and a light footfall running quickly through the yard. He knew it was Eugenia. He felt her drop on her knees beside him. She lifted his head tenderly, resting it in her lap, saying over her shoulder, "Good Lord! Father! What has happened?!"

" I must have run over his foot..." Bending a little closer, he said apologetically, "My dear Lawrence, I'm terribly sorry."

Eugenia, who was apparently unmindful of proprieties during medical emergencies, felt her way down the lower part of Lawrence's leg in an attempt to reach his injured foot.

Lawrence opened his eyes and squinted up. Three heads, and what appeared to be six pairs of eyes, swam above him. With a groan, Lawrence quickly shut his eyes again and slowly sat up, feeling for his injured foot. Thank heaven it was his weaker leg. It would heal, and he'd still have his strong leg to rely on. He leaned back, to be supported unnecessarily, but quite sweetly, by Eugenia, who had scooted closer, and was even now gently smoothing his hair from his forehead. After all, what need was there to reject this welcomed closeness?

Mrs. Merritt came bustling from the house with Mr. Cavendish barking excitedly at her heels. "Good gracious! What has happened?" she demanded, quickly scanning the scene. Mr. Cavendish tried frantically to get past Eugenia's restraining hand to lick Lawrence's face.

"I- I misjudged my wheels, madam mine, and… accidentally ran over Lawrence's foot." confessed Mr. Merritt. He mopped his brow again. Mrs. Merritt's mouth fell open as she stared at her husband in amazement. Then her attention was captured by Lawrence and Eugenia.

Eugenia sat on the ground behind Lawrence. He was propped up against her knee, and her arm encircled his shoulders. She was absent-mindedly, or so it appeared, stroking his forehead with her free hand. She had a familiar no-nonsense look about her; her brows were creased, her neck stiff, and her mouth straight. Her mother knew that expression. Her daughter was beginning a medical interrogation.

"Where does it hurt the worst, Mr. Trellaway?"

"My foot."

"I know that," she nearly sputtered, "I am asking for more details!" Lawrence found it cheered him considerably to provoke her. Maybe it was worth the pain.

Eugenia glanced up. "Captain Fortescue, would you mind taking off Lawrence's boot so very much?"

At that, Lawrence sat up hastily on his own and fanned his hands out protectively over his injured foot. "I will do it myself! I have faced much worse." Taking a deep breath, he reached down to his heel, loosened the boot, and began to remove it slowly. It was excruciating but he bit his lip and finished the job with a ruthless tug. Almost before he could look at it himself, Eugenia was bent over it, pulling off his stocking and asking him to bend this or that toe.

Mrs. Merritt popped up and pulled her husband to stand with her. Lawrence heard her say, "Nothing more to be done here, Merritt. If you want to make yourself useful, you should stop on your way to the solicitor's office and tell Lawrence's parents what has happened and have them send a carriage for him."

Lawrence interrupted as best he could from the ground behind them.

"I beg your pardon, but I have a horse here. He is perfectly sound though I am not. There is no reason that I cannot ride home. Fortescue will help me as I need it. I assure you, I will be fine."

The Merritts both turned to look at Lawrence, then Mrs. Merritt grew peculiarly animated and practically shoved her husband back onto the seat of the gig, turning to shout over her shoulder to Lawrence.

"You are right, of course. We will deal nicely without Mr. Merritt. He simply must not delay! Captain Fortescue, I am afraid that anything that you may have had to discuss with Mr. Merritt must now wait for another time. That is, if there was anything in particular that you were hoping to discuss. Today is decidedly not the day for it. Not after this."

"Of course, madam." Fortescue had stood while being addressed and now made a polite bow. He had a hint of a smile playing about his lips, but he did his best to add solemnity to his voice as he said, "Certainly. I should not think of it. I have come only to say that I will soon be leaving Cherrybrook."

If Fortescue had thought that the Merritts would take this news in their stride, he was mistaken, but nor could he determine exactly in what spirit his announcement had been received or interpreted.

Frozen in action, Mr. Merritt's hands held the lines taut, and his driving whip hovered over his head, all the crack taken out of it for now. He gave a sort of a shudder and rested his hands on his knees. He glanced down at his lap and then looked back at the young men and, addressing himself to Fortescue, said, "That is news, indeed." He dropped his chin and looked as though he did not know what to say. There was a moment of strained silence, then he said, "I... I hope that you will return soon and pay us a visit."

Mr. Merritt studied Lawrence afresh, his eyes full of concern, "And you are sure that you will fully recover? Are you quite certain?"

Lawrence opened his mouth to respond but Eugenia interjected, "Yes, at worst it is probably a fracture or a broken toe," Eugenia had taken her place behind Lawrie again, his self-appointed support, and added, "With rest he should be his old self again soon. But, Papa, I cannot understand how you could have made such a blunder!"

To Lawrence, Eugenia added, "I promise to check on you every day. I feel as though this is quite my fault!"

"Now, my pet, it was not you. Certainly not," said Mrs. Merritt, who was hovering near her daughter and Lawrence.

She cast a waspish look at her husband before turning to Captain Fortescue. Mrs. Merritt's expression softened like butter in the sun, and she seemed to smile more warmly than before. In fact, she came right up to the gentleman and tilted her head prettily (doubtlessly an art she had employed in her courtship with Mr. Merritt), and said with considerable sweetness, "My dear Captain, we are so sorry to hear you are leaving us. I daresay that Cherrybrook will seem desolate without you." In a mollifying tone, she added, "But I am sure that in time you would have found that we are far, far too dull for you."

"Not that, madam... never dull," Fortescue assured her kindly.

Lawrence watched the Merritts curiously. His parents' friends seemed to be acting peculiarly, but no serious complaints troubled his mind, for he had discovered he had only to knit his brows and wince the tiniest bit and Eugenia held him more tightly.

Finally, Mr. Merritt gave a parting goodbye and drove from the yard and down the road in the direction of town.

There was a big fuss made of moving Lawrence to the parlour. Fortescue provided a strong shoulder to lean on, and Lawrence hobbled into the house with the women fluttering ahead with his hat and walking stick.

When Lawrence was led to a settee, Eugenia had already stacked several pillows nearby with which to prop up his foot. When he lowered himself, she gently lifted his leg and began stuffing pillows beneath it.

Lawrence observed her energetic care with gratitude and some amazement. It was true Eugenia did not seem in the least bit sick. She seemed cheerful and entirely at ease, healthier and more beautiful than he had ever seen her.

Fortescue also seemed to notice this, for he stood quietly off to one side, hat in hand, with an amused smile touching his lips. Eugenia seemed to have entirely forgotten his presence in the small room.

Lawrence felt no small amount of relief that Mrs. Merritt had neither flown into a rage nor rushed for her smelling salts over Fortescue's announcement. She, and indeed Mr. Merritt and Eugenia, had every right to be offended by John's boldness and overt acts of courtship. If Eugenia were any other girl, she would likely be begging John to stay with tears and entreaties, but she did not.

Instead, when Mr. Trellaway arrived, Eugenia leaned over Lawrie (which quite caused his pulse to race) to look out of the window that faced the road. She rose and strode purposefully toward Fortescue, extending her hand to him in a manner a young woman might use if she were an old school friend, or even (a lowering thought) a sister, rather than an aggrieved lady who had just had her heart broken.

"Captain Fortescue," she said sweetly and with a small curtsy, "thank you for the good pleasure of your company these past weeks." She blushed very slightly. "I hope... I wish you every happiness... and do come see us again won't you, all of us here in Cherrybrook?"

Fortescue, an arrested grin on his face, turned momentarily to Lawrence before replying, "I hope to, indeed. I believe you will find Trellaway a most tractable patient. I want you to know, Miss Merritt, that I hold you in high regard and feel certain that I do right in trusting my good friend to your expert care." This last part of his speech was delivered with all the seriousness of a surgeon.

There was no time for Eugenia to offer a response, for at that moment Lawrence's father entered the house with a cursory knock. He swept his hat from his head and bowed to the ladies of the house as he strode across the room to Lawrie's side.

"What's got you laid up then, Lawrence? A bruised foot? That will keep you off the dance floor for certain, which should be to your liking." His father winked, then turned to Eugenia. "What do you think, Miss Merritt? Will he mend?"

"Oh yes, I think he will be back on his feet again soon if he keeps his foot elevated for a few days." Eugenia looked up at Mr. Trellaway and implored "May I have your permission to visit to check on your son's progress?"

Mr. Trellaway smiled indulgently at Eugenia. "I am sure we would all be most grateful."

Lawrence opened his mouth to protest but then recalled that he had very recently been cradled in her lap and hadn't exactly been repulsed by Eugenia's tender assistance. But as he did not want to cause trouble, or stir anyone to pity, he said instead, "Thank you, but I cannot imagine that I'll need much attending, so come only when it is convenient for you to do so."

Eugenia lifted her brows and smiled sweetly at him. He was strongly reminded of her as a young girl, when she had looked tractable yet acted according to her own wishes.

"Then you may expect me tomorrow," she said sunnily.

Lawrie's father shot his son an approving glance from under his bushy brows, before motioning to the captain, saying, "Give me a hand here, won't you, Fortescue?". Between the two men, a protesting Lawrence donned his hat and was hefted to his feet, then swiftly propelled out the door held open by Mrs. Merritt.

Eugenia and her mother stood on the front steps and watched as Lawrence was helped up onto the seat of the gig. Before sitting, he stood gingerly on one foot, and removing his hat, waved to the women. With a smile, Eugenia caught her lower lip between her teeth and sighed contentedly as she waved back. When the men were seated, Mr. Trellaway urged the carriage horse forward.

A little way behind them, Fortescue mounted his horse and took the reins of Lawrie's chestnut mare to lead her home. He leaned forward and cued his horse to go, and as they left the yard, the captain swept off his hat and gave Eugenia a winsome grin.

She waved in return.

Her mother said with a relieved smile and sparkling eyes, "I cannot believe Captain Fortescue did not turn your head, Eugenia. You must be quite the most strong-minded girl in England."

Chapter Eight

Early the following day, despite Lawrence's objections that it was too precipitous, Captain John Fortescue prepared to leave. "I shall see you at the wedding, and I expect it won't be long in coming. And if," he said with a smile that belied his murderous tone, "you are unable to secure a future with Miss Merritt, my friend, I'll eat my hat... and come back to ask for her hand myself!"

Lawrence swatted him, "Be off with you, fool."

Every attempt Lawrence had made to hobble around the house that day was bitterly resisted, and while he had managed to brush off his nurses during the first part of the day, and bid a fond farewell to Captain Fortescue, he was happy to lie down and let his head roll back against the cushions. He soon became heavy-eyed, and had very nearly nodded off to sleep when he heard a small commotion in the front hall.

A perfunctory rap on the door announced the entrance of Dobson, who, looking apologetic and slightly disapproving, said, "Sir, Miss Merritt is asking to see you." He hesitated, and added, "She does have her maid with her, should your mother be unavailable."

"Thank you, Dobson." Lawrence swung his legs off the sofa and barely had time to run a hand through his hair before Eugenia and her maid came spilling into the room.

"Mr. Trellaway." Eugenia bowed her head politely as she approached him. She was rosy from her walk and her blue eyes sparkled with light. Lawrie thought he had never seen her look lovelier. She was wearing a pale, jonquil dress, and although it was slightly faded, it did her no disservice. As she untied her bonnet strings, she admonished, "Just one day after your accident, I find you sitting with your foot down! If you want to heal properly, you must do as I say." She took off her bonnet and set it on the small table next to Lawrence's elbow. "Keep your foot elevated. That is the first rule." She frowned a little at his swollen foot. "Why, there is no reason that you cannot be doing so this minute." Looking around the room, her gaze lit upon one of Mrs. Trellaway's soft chairs. "Mary? Do fetch me the pillow from that chair. Yes, that's the one. Now, Mr. Trellaway, let me lift that foot of yours and have a look at it."

"I absolutely will not agree to that scheme today! Yesterday was one thing, but today is quite different." Lawrence had a mulish look about his jaw, and professed, "I will be fine; I have looked at it myself."

"If it is indeed fine, why will you not let me examine it?"

"Because it is swollen and looks shockingly hideous, and I refuse to let you...." Here he broke off. As Eugenia began to object and reach for his foot, Lawrie snatched her hand and held it in a firm grasp. Their eyes met. Just then the sound of his mother's footsteps reached their ears, and he reluctantly released her hand and let her pull free. Mrs. Trellaway entered the room, saying cheerfully, "Oh welcome, my dear Eugenia! I suppose you have heard that Captain Fortescue has left us?"

"Why, yes. Mrs. Trellaway. He and your son were together at our home yesterday when my father ran over your son's foot. I cannot imagine how it happened! Our mare is normally so docile." Eugenia bit the inside of her cheek and glanced nervously at Lawrie. "In any event, I am here to apologise afresh and check on Lawr- Mr. Trellaway."

"That's very thoughtful of you, child." gushed his mother. "We can be thankful that Lawrence will recover quickly. A man with military honours, after all, is strong."

"Yes, ma'am. I should think so."

Mrs. Trellaway bustled about the room, opening the drapes a little wider, straightening the folds, doing inconsequential tidying which had almost certainly been done within the last two days if not the last two hours.

At last Lawrence's feelings overcame him. He despised feeling so helpless, and he told Eugenia as much with some asperity. "I will not pretend that I do not enjoy your attention and concern, Miss Merritt, but I can only accept this visit of yours with any degree of dignity if you promise me that you feel no pity. I cannot bear to be pitied" he declared vehemently. "I feel that my limp is more than enough to make me a poor dance partner. In addition, if you were to make repeated nursing visits, I should not want it marked and for your visits to become the subject of local gossip."

Mrs. Trellaway stifled a squeak and set a vase down with rather more force than necessary. She shook her head slightly and pursed her lips as if in warning that he would best shut *his* lips as tightly and not ruin anything.

Eugenia, who had been sitting quite close to Lawrie, her skirted bottom lightly touching his thigh, stiffened perceptibly at his words. She scooted forward slightly so they were no longer touching, and sat primly on the edge of the chaise lounge, her hands in her lap. As he watched, she withdrew, her normally pliant, smiling mouth straightened like a reed, and a steely look came into her eyes as she focused on the wall directly in front of her.

Mrs. Trellaway walked to the foot of the lounge where the pair sat and she leaned into Eugenia's line of sight, saying, "Cook opened a jar of peach preserves, and you simply must try some. I'll have tea fetched."

"Oh, thank you, dear Mrs. Trellaway, but I shan't stay that long. I am obviously imposing upon your son's time."

Forgetting himself, Lawrence turned back to her and said sardonically, "Eugenia, don't be a goose! You are not imposing. Not unless the Pratchetts' sick cow needs you more badly than I do, a soldier with a poor leg."

She rounded on him with eyes wide, "Mr. Trellaway! How dare you accuse me of confusing you, or in any way equating you with my animal patients! You have made far more of your limp than anyone else, and I begin to think you feel quite sorry for yourself. The real damage from the war must be inside you, Lieutenant. Your gait irregularity does not even begin to signify."

"I will fetch tea!" declared Mrs. Trellaway in an unnaturally high-pitched voice. She slipped from the room before anyone could object.

"I am ashamed then, Miss Merritt. I had not realised that my attitude was so obvious and affecting. I should not want it to colour our friendship."

Thinking that to remind Eugenia of her own previous promise of friendship must certainly comfort her after such a confession, it seemed instead to have the opposite effect.

"You have marked my words too carefully, Mr. Trell-away," she murmured. "I will say no more today as I have said quite enough already. I am embarrassed to have been so transparent with you."

She was uncommonly pretty, sitting here next to him with the sun filtering in through the window. He had a reckless impulse to make a declaration but decided that he most certainly had better wait until he was at least able to stand up on his own.

"Please Miss Merritt, do not apologise for honesty. Ever. Maybe it's the way of most people to hide their true opinions, but it is, I think, not the way of you and me. He took her hand gently in his, his eyes filled with warmth as he searched hers. "Let us start over, fresh and new. Let's put aside our parents' hopes, all expectations, our own misunderstandings, and try now to learn our own minds.... our own hearts."

Eugenia's eyes warmed at this, and she tilted her head as she gazed at him. There was a slight up curve in the corner of her mouth, and she said, "Very well. I like your suggestion, and while I do not pretend to understand your precise meaning, I do agree that I should like to begin our friendship afresh."

"Tea!" rang out Mrs. Trellaway's voice just before the door opened and she popped back into the room.

Eugenia's shoulders slumped slightly forward, perhaps in disappointment at this untimely interruption, but she smoothed her skirts and moved to a nearby chair where she graciously accepted the steaming cup. "I believe I do have just enough time to sample your preserves, after all.... thank you, ma'am," she smiled.

The days of Lawrence's recovery passed quickly. Eugenia visited the Trellaways' home frequently, often in the company of her father and Mr. Cavendish, upon both of whom Mrs. Trellaway lavished treats. Eugenia brought Lawrence reports on the state of her garden efforts, of local animal health emergencies to which she'd been called, and of town news. They talked of Browning and Wordsworth. Once, she brought her injured rabbit, now restored to fitness and bundled into a basket with the lid tied down, to bid Lawrence goodbye before she released the creature into its more natural surroundings of the nearby woodland thickets.

No matter the topic, or how comfortably they conversed, laughed, or amiably disagreed, Eugenia never sat as close to him as she had done the day after the accident. Lawrence was acutely aware of this intentional abstinence. Although he understood the dictates of propriety concerning young ladies, he knew Eugenia to be unconventional, and without artifice, even sometimes contemptuous of these social strictures. He noticed that she was careful not to touch his fingers when handing him tea, or a pen. This physical neglect both tormented and thrilled him. It was undeniable that Eugenia was happy in his company; she had developed a rosy glow about her, and her eyes shone when they met his over the pages of a book. But her continued guard over their physical space made it difficult for Lawrence to divine what place, if any, he held in her heart. "Am I still just a neighbour?" he asked himself, "a loyal family friend, like Mr. Cavendish?" He could not wait much longer to find out. His nights were becoming less than restful, for thoughts of her kept him awake and miserable. His dearest hope was that Eugenia was suffering the same powerful distraction.

Chapter Nine

She was suffering. Left to herself in her garden, or in her bed at night, Eugenia had much the same malady as Lawrence, only worse. While Lawrence had nothing to regret in things he'd said to her since his return (or so it seemed to her), she now very much regretted telling Lawrie how "comfortable" she was in his presence, and how "nice" it was to "have a friend and no husband." She could hardly say she was comfortable now.

His words, "I should not want it to colour our friendship" were burned into her memory. It must be that she had convinced him that she wished only to be his friend and she found she did not want to risk losing the recently acquired closeness by attempting to make something more of it.

No, what this situation called for was propriety. Remembering keenly the effect that he'd had on her pulse when they had touched in the past, she was now making all attempts to avoid any physical contact. It was not natural for Eugenia to be so restrained. She was affectionate and passionate by nature, and she found one hundred ways in which she was used to breaking the rules of propriety. She did not know how much longer she could bear it.

Eugenia pictured the way Lawrence's face seemed to brighten when she came into view. She did not believe that she imagined this. Also, he seemed easy around her speaking and listening comfortably. She adored the way he propped his chin on his hand, one finger crooked over his lips, and blinked slowly as he listened, really listened, to what she had to say. Eugenia sometimes was afraid that Lawrence could hear her heart pounding when they sat together, or that she might lose herself in his blue eyes and betray too much emotion of her own, so she purposefully introduced topics about science articles, or crop rotations, steam travel, anything to keep her mind diverted from the truth: she was deeply in love with Lawrence Trellaway.

Eugenia had donned her favourite gardening dress, apron and straw bonnet one particularly fine morning, and was about to harvest herbs for drying, when her mother burst through the back door, her ample breast bouncing as she trotted to where Eugenia stood at the garden gate, gesturing wildly to Eugenia to come near. When she was within earshot, she whispered excitedly, "Eugenia...!"

She stopped. "Good gracious, girl. And you in your faded green muslin and apron, and... oh, well, it can't be helped!"

Eugenia glanced down and laughed, "Mother, whatever is it?"

"It's young Mr. Trellaway.... Lawrence!" He's come all this way to call, and on foot, my dear!" Mrs. Merritt clasped her hands together. "Thank Heaven he is fully recovered."

Eugenia, who had her own suspicions about what had happened on the day her father had rolled over Lawrie's foot, replied rather sharply as she untied her apron with shaking fingers, "What a relief that our gig was no heavier!"

Her mother seemed to be in a completely abstracted state. "Do you suppose he'd like a strawberry tart, or perh aps... Oh! Never mind." She side-stepped back toward the kitchen door. "I think Hart has just seen him inside! I hear the front door closing. If he wants to speak with you, shall I ...? Would you like me to...?"

"Yes, Mother," Eugenia replied with a choke, hurriedly trying to peel off her apron, and craning her neck to look toward the house. "Yes, of course. Show him through to the garden, won't you?"

As soon as her mother was out of sight, Eugenia smoothed her hair and took several deep breaths with her eyes closed and held her stomach. This was the first time that Lawrence had called upon her family since his injury. Perhaps it meant nothing; but then again, perhaps it meant something.

Lawrence was met by a very cheerful Mrs. Merritt. "Dear Lawrence! My, my! How very good to see you walking again! Come in, come in....pray, be seated, no... wait." She paused and asked tentatively, "Are you here to see my husband or Eugenia?"

"I think perhaps I will see Miss Merritt first, and Mr. Merritt after," he replied.

Mrs. Merritt nearly jumped to show him through the house to the garden. "She's in the herbs," said the lady of the house as she opened the back door and ushered him into the garden.

This statement struck Lawrence as exquisitely humorous. With dancing eyes, he thanked her cordially for saving him from an unnecessary search, and he made his way carefully down the steps to the garden.

He did, indeed, find Eugenia in the herb garden, standing in the bordering elder flowers. She smiled and waved as Lawrence picked his way along the path, his progress impeded somewhat by Mr. Cavendish, who barked and jumped at his legs and walking stick. He bent down to pet the little dog, ruffling up his hair affectionately, before addressing Eugenia. "Miss Merritt! How are you on this fine day?"

"I am very well, thank you... and so pleased! Did you walk this entire way?" she asked with apparent surprise and pleasure.

Lawrence nodded and stood a few paces back, his free hand in his pocket. "I did, yes. I've been pushing myself to walk further and further every day out of your concerned eyeshot, and feel I am next to being fully restored." He hesitated, then asked, "Miss Merritt, do you have time to talk... or do I interrupt you?"

Lawrence was heartened to see that Eugenia was flustered and blushing profusely. This gave him courage to press his suit.

He took a couple steps closer. "Do you think your mother is watching us?"

"Undoubtedly," said Eugenia without looking at the house.

"Ah, yes. Is it possible for her to hear us?"

"I don't believe so, but if you'd like, follow me here, we will have a little more privacy." Eugenia led him back just beyond a small hedgerow and he set down his walking stick. She looked up at him anxiously. "What did you want to say? You seldom begin a conversation on such a serious note."

Lawrence gazed down at his toes for a moment, then smiled gently at Eugenia. "I wonder if you are capable of putting something out of its misery, Miss Merritt?"

Eugenia's hand flew to her breast, and she looked at him searchingly. "Not an animal?"

Realising he'd made a very poor start of it, Lawrence quickly added, "The miserable creature I am speaking of is me." He looked at her without blinking.

Still with confusion in her eyes, Eugenia took a step closer to him. "Why do you say you are miserable?"

"You and I agreed that we should begin our friendship again, but I find myself increasingly wretched, yet you seem just as happy as you were before." He hesitated a moment before continuing. "Eugenia, are you so glad to be rid of all suitors then?"

She looked down at the ground, her brows knitted together and her foot tapping, but she did not walk away. Lawrie closed his eyes for a moment in profound relief before continuing. "Is it...? Could it be that you did not want them to be right about us? Our parents?"

"Yes!" She blurted. "It sounds terribly absurd and not a little prideful to confess it, but yes! Besides, I had got used to the idea of being independent. With so much to occupy my time: this garden, my pets, injured animals, learning how to run the household, and..." Here she paused and bit her lip, carefully scrutinising Lawrence's face before finishing with, "livestock management."

"Do you expect that to shock me? For it does not." He waited while Eugenia chased a pebble with her boot. Then she folded her arms and slowly lifted anxious eyes to his.

"I didn't think I was capable of..." here she faltered and almost didn't continue, but the look on Lawrie's face told her that she would need to speak honestly or risk losing him. He would not play games. "I did not think I could love a man in such a way."

"In what way is that?" he teased. He took a step closer. "You, who boldly lecture upon the latest livestock breeding techniques, even in mixed company, cannot speak now of love without blushing, is that it?" he chuckled.

Her bonneted head bobbed up and down, until she froze mid-bob and covered her mouth with her hands to stifle a weak scream. She looked at Lawrie with eyes as round as sunflowers, and with a little jump, she started to move away from him. Lawrie grabbed her wrist and pulled her back to face him. "What's this? What are you thinking now, you silly chit?" But he spoke teasingly, half his mouth was turned up in a crooked smile. "Now, you as good as confess that you love me, or likely could - and then you bolt?"

"But Lawrie - good gracious! I've done it again! What a blunder I'm making of this! Now I've gone and called you by your name. I've referred to you always as Lawrie... like when we were but children. Besides, I hear your mother talk about you, and she calls you Lawrie, and..." She might have gone on and on, babbling and gesturing wildly with her free hand, but Lawrie put a restraining finger lightly to her lips.

He pulled her nearer until his face was inches from hers.

"Stop your sorry raving and attend to me. Do I look like an offended gentleman?"

Eugenia, now silenced, slowly lifted her gaze to meet his. Lawrie's expression shone with good humour and something else, a spark of something that might have seemed a bit wild, even dangerous in another man's face. What she read in his eyes prompted an answering glint in her own as she replied, "If you mean by that question, do you appear offended, 'no' is what I shall say. But, sir, if you are asking whether you look like a gentleman, the answer is also 'no!'. You look like a man who is about to..." Before finishing her sentence, she clapped her hands over her mouth.

"No? I do not look the perfect gentleman and friend? You seem to know exactly what I am about to profess."

"But Lawrie! I've put everything topsy-turvy again. I wasn't supposed to be the one who... who..." She said this so balefully that Lawrie took pity on her and silenced her by kissing her softly, tentatively, then slowly pulling away. Eugenia blinked. "Oh!" she whispered.

Lawrie cleared his throat. "Miss Eugenia Merritt, before you propose marriage to me by accident, please do me the honour of hearing me." He dropped his hands from Eugenia's arms and twined his fingers in hers. "Eugenia, please accept my hand in marriage, for I do love you devotedly. You'll make me the happiest of men if you say 'yes'."

Eugenia felt a wave of heat and nervousness flutter through her. It started with her hand, the one Lawrie was holding, and travelled up to her head and down to her toes. She'd never felt so pleasantly affected in all her life.

Pretending that she needed to consider his offer before replying, Eugenia reached her free hand up to his collar and asked, "Will you let me keep pets in the house?"

"Of course," he answered, smiling.

"Do you agree to share the responsibilities of farm and estate management with me?" She walked her finger up around his neck and he smiled lazily and blinked his sky-blue eyes slowly.

"I doubt I could do nearly so well without your expert opinions," he replied.

She tugged his head down a little so that their foreheads were touching. "Can we fill our home with cherubic babies?" she asked shyly.

Lawrie raised his eyebrows. "Oh, absolutely - or we can certainly try," and he gave her a devastating grin.

"All right. I accept!"

Lawrie pulled her close.

"Kiss me," said Lawrence, and Eugenia did.

Epilogue

"Well, Merritt," said Mr. Albert Trellaway to his friend, "we did it."

Mr. Gregory Merritt smiled ruefully but shook his head. "No. They did it. I very nearly undid it, despite my warning to you on the very subject of succumbing to the temptation of subterfuge."

"It was unnerving, I grant you that. Having Fortescue sweep in like that, just when we expected everything to proceed easily." Trellaway tapped his glass.

Mr. Merritt gave a guffaw and picked up his glass. "I am Eugenia's father. I never thought it would go easily, but I should not have panicked."

Mr. Trellaway rose to a stand and held his glass high in the air, "A toast to friends and family!"

"Aye," said Mr. Merritt, rising and meeting his glass with Trellaway's in a satisfying clink. "To friends, family, and new beginnings!"

The End

Thank you for reading!

D id you enjoy Lawrie and Eugenia's love story? I *do* hope so!

If so, please leave me a descriptive positive review. Not only does your review help me as an author, it also helps readers with taste similar to yours find books they'll enjoy.

Discover more books by Charlotte at www.charlottebrot hersauthor.com

Please join my mailing list! Book friends will always be the first to receive free goodies and special offers :-).

Bonus Prologue

Welcome to "A Fair-Weather Friend", the 2nd book in the Cherrybrook year series!

Where has he gone?" John Talbot clenched his fists but stopped short of any further display of anger in the presence of his mother.

Mrs. Talbot sat on the front half of an amply proportioned, high-backed chair and watched nervously as her eldest son turned away from her and resumed pacing the length of the long, narrow room.

John ran his fingers through his unfashionably close-trimmed, light brown hair in vexed distraction as he wrestled with his thoughts. Finally, he stopped abruptly across the table from where she sat and planted his hands firmly on the tabletop. Leaning forward he said, "Mother, may I ask why you allowed our uncle to be drawn into this? I thought we had agreed to spare your family our embarrassments."

Mrs. Talbot looked down at her lap for a moment before raising tearful eyes to John's. She said simply, "Jonas asked me if I did not think it a fine idea for him to start in his uncle's office, and… and without asking *me* to approach Carlton on his behalf, he wrote to my brother directly." She frowned. "But John, I cannot shake the hope that this will be the experience that will make him a responsible man. Is it really so terrible?"

John let the breath out slowly and made as near a growling sound as a gentleman could be accused of.

"You realise that he may bring trouble, not only upon himself, but upon Uncle Jennings? Jonas has a way of causing grief wherever he goes." He dropped his head for a moment and then raised it again and gazed sadly at his mother. "I wish you would have warned the Jennings off, and encouraged them to refuse him."

"How can you expect me to deny Jonas? He is still my son, despite his past regrettable behaviour." She paused. "There will be very few of the sorts of diversions in Cherrybrook that he was inclined to enjoy in Town. And besides," she grew animated, "did you yourself not agree that, after Jonas returned from London this last time, he was quite scholarly, always walking about the house with some journal or other or his father's Debrett's and Burke's Peerage? He stayed up late several nights with books and letters scattered all about. He seemed to be quite industrious."

John Talbot nodded slowly and walked thoughtfully around the table until he stood behind his mother's chair and rested his right hand gently on her shoulder.

She fought back tears and patted his wide strong hand with her thin, ladylike one without looking up.

John squeezed her shoulder consolingly, and his voice was softer and quieter when he next spoke. "I'll put to rights anything that Jonas upsets." He paused for a moment, then said, " Perhaps you are correct, and this apprenticeship will prove he is applying himself at last."

Mrs. Talbot turned around to face her son and dabbed at her eyes with a napkin. "Do I look as though I have cried? I shouldn't want your brothers to be troubled when they come downstairs."

"You look right as rain, Mother. Try to put our distress from your mind."

John smiled grimly and strode purposefully from the dining parlour into the front hall, his willowy mother trailing along behind him. He took his hat from the hatrack. "Do not fret yourself. I will be back on the shy side of an hour. I am going for a walk and will return before supper." He put on his hat and straightened his jacket. With a nod, he left out the front door, shutting it loudly behind him.

Mrs. Talbot walked quickly back to the dining parlour, straight to the window that faced the road, and watched her stalwart son trudge off the left, the way that most quickly led to the countryside and solitude.

She knew it was not proper that John carried so much of the family burden. Cynicism and worry were already etched into his face. If she had not known his age, she might have thought him nearer forty than thirty.

Bonus Chapter One

*T*oday is an exceptional day,

mused Miss Marian Lyle. Not because it was a sun-filled Sunday morning, and she was sitting in a pew near the front of Cherrybrook's Holy Cross Church, for as eldest daughter of the vicar, she was nearly always in attendance. No. Today was exceptional because she knew that two rows behind her sat Mr. Jonas Talbot, the visiting nephew of their respected local solicitor, Mr. Jennings.

Marian trained her attention forward and forced herself to take a deep breath. She closed her eyes and enjoyed the elevating sensation of a sunbeam warming her face as it shone down through the high, stained-glass window of Christ, the Good Shepherd.

Her serenity was short-lived. Esther, one of her sisters, elbowed her sharply in the ribs and frowned at her meaningfully. Younger than she by three years, Esther was sitting as straight as a rod and had her eyes opened wide with an expression clearly meant as an admonition for Marian to stay awake. *As if I would fall asleep today of all days.* Marian inhaled again slowly and silently recited the closing scripture in time with her father.

Finally came the benediction, and Marian, Esther, their mother, and the two youngest Lyles, stood with the rest of the congregation and the chapel began to empty.

Marian slightly shifted her position so that she could see the people behind her. Immediately she spotted her query near the centre of the nave. Mr. Talbot. He was somewhat tall with graceful, long limbs and a narrow, elegant face. His hair and eyes were dark, his brows expressive. His curious gaze fleetingly met hers before the Jennings ushered him out of their family pew and down the aisle.

Soon the old, stone church was nearly emptied, and though the Reverend Mr. Lyle was still engaged in conversation with Lord and Lady Hamblin, the church's most distinguished parishioners, Marian and the rest of the Lyle family made their way through the nave and out into the shade of the churchyard.

Glancing again in Mr. Talbot's direction, Marian agreed with her former opinion that he was quite handsome. He had a pleasant face and easy manners. As she judiciously studied him from across the lawn, he seemed to grow restless in his conversation with Mrs. Jennings and Mrs. Walpole and began to look around.

Marian did not want the subject of her curiosity to discover that she had been watching him. She looked away quickly and clutched Esther's arm. Understandably, her sister's reaction was one of alarm, so Marian pressed in closer and whispered severely, "*Do* try to look like we're engaged in a conversation that you are enjoying. You look as though you have just bitten into a green apple!"

"Why-" then Esther, spotting the subject of her sister's interest, said in a nervous falsetto, "Oh! I understand now. Why did you not tell me that—Oh! He is walking toward us!"

Marian had just enough time to hiss "Stop squealing!" before he was within probable earshot.

Removing his hat politely, the young man stepped near, and addressed himself to Marian and Esther. "Excuse me, ladies," he said on a note of apology, "I shall have someone introduce us properly as soon as opportunity permits. But I have it upon reliable authority," here he glanced significantly back at his aunt and continued with a relaxed grin, "that you are Miss Lyle and Miss Esther Lyle. You are certainly acquainted with Mr. and Mrs. Jennings? I am their nephew, Jonas Talbot."

Esther began to say, "Oh, we know who you...'"

Marian cut in hastily, "We know Mr. and Mrs. Jennings well, of course. They had mentioned that a nephew was soon to arrive in Cherrybrook."

From the corner of her eye, Marian could see her mother fast approaching. When Mrs. Lyle had apprehended them, Mr. Talbot stepped back a pace, and bowed handsomely to her. Then, with a quick smile that encompassed all three ladies, he began again, "You are the vicar's family?"

"Yes," responded her mother. "I am the missus, and this is our eldest, Miss Marian Lyle," she said with a light touch to Marian's shoulder, "and her sister, Esther. I do not see their younger sister and brother at present," she said, briefly scanning the churchyard.

Jonas Talbot sparkled at Marian as his eyes met hers, and she felt her cheeks grow unaccountably warm.

He gave a quick nod of acknowledgement to Esther, then looked to Mrs. Lyle. "What a good sermon your husband has given us, ma'am. I have always felt we can never be reminded often enough to use our talents wisely."

Mrs. Lyle inclined her head and responded stiffly, "Then I will say that it is good to hear that my husband's words have fallen on fertile soil."

There was a moment of strained silence before Marian said, "Mama, this is Mr. Jonas Talbot. He is Mr. Jennings' nephew who has come to visit," she looked at Mr. Talbot questioningly, "for some duration?"

Mrs. Lyle examined the young man before her. She must have been convinced of his open countenance for when she spoke again, there was more warmth in her voice. "The Jennings' nephew? Well then, we are happy to welcome you. What business brings you to Cherrybrook, Mr. Talbot?" inquired Mrs. Lyle, "Or are you here purely for the pleasure of visiting your aunt and uncle?"

"I have just finished reading law, but have come down most recently from my family home in Pinnset." Mr. Talbot rubbed his jaw thoughtfully. "Like Mr. Jennings, I intend to set up a firm of my own. But I might," he added,"read in chambers to become a barrister. But that is neither here nor there," he said with a hesitant smile. "Regardless, my uncle has kindly offered to have me here and give me a start."

Mrs. Lyle smiled approvingly at Mr. Talbot and then beamed at her daughters. "I think law is an admirable line of work. Think of all the good you can do for others."

"Quite right," concurred Mr. Talbot, his eyes opening widely in surprise. "Of course. That is why I chose such a path. Well, that and the strong influence of my father."

"Your father also practises law?"

"*Practised*. My father is no longer living." Mr. Talbot frowned and looked down for a moment before continuing. "He died about this same time last year."

"I am sorry to hear about the loss of your father," said Mrs. Lyle with tenderness, inclining her head. "So very hard on the family, I always think," she sighed. Seeing that Mr. Talbot had frowned slightly, she abruptly changed to a more cheerful subject. "Well... we shall all look forward to inviting you to our home. Would you care to join us for dinner this Thursday? We live just there in the vicarage," said Mrs. Lyle with a nod at the nearest house.

Jonas looked over his shoulder in the direction she had indicated. Their large, tidy, stone and timber home stood on the other side of a thick row of lilacs, its rough surface glowing warmly in the sun. The lilac bushes separated the house from the churchyard. Beyond the lilacs and behind the house, several ancient but well-tended apple trees rose up against a fence that separated the little orchard from the church cemetery.

"Ah! A very fine house, indeed." Mr. Talbot smiled as he glanced fleetingly at Marian before turning to her mother. "Madam, you are too kind," he said with a polite bow. "I am happy to accept your dinner invitation."

Mrs. Lyle nodded with finality. "Then it is settled. We shall expect you on Thursday." Her gaze drifted back to the small crowd still gathered near the open doors of the church, and she held up a gloved hand to block the sun while she looked. Her eyes brightened when she found Mr. and Mrs. Jennings. "I would very much like to invite your aunt and uncle as well. Let us walk together and invite them, shall we?""An excellent idea," agreed Mr. Talbot, and he offered Mrs. Lyle his arm, which she took. With Marian and Esther following close behind, they set off across the church green to invite the Jennings to dinner.

Mr. and Mrs. Jennings cheerfully accepted the offer and, plans having been amicably settled, that cheerful, round couple and their tall, thin nephew took leave of them. Marian walked a few paces away from the others and watched the handsome Mr. Talbot stride away, down the gentle green slope. Her heart skipped a beat when she was rewarded by one last look from him before he stepped onto the main road. Marian's hand flew inadvertently to her chest, and she sighed happily.

"Was that Mr. Jennings' nephew?" asked a familiar and beloved female voice at her shoulder a few moments later.

"Yes. Yes, it was," Marian smiled with a hint of pride. Her dearest friend, Eugenia Merritt, stepped nearer and slid her arm through hers, an excited, quizzing look in her eye.

"Well? What did he say? What did *you* say?"she questioned. "I must say that to me, it looked as though he singled you out! The only other ladies he talked to were Mrs. Kent and the Misses Kent, and since he was sitting behind the Kents in church, he could hardly ignore them even if he wanted to, could he?"

The Kent sisters, Angela and Teresa, were not favourites with either Marian or Eugenia. Their sharp eyes and noses were often in everyone else's private matters, and on several occasions in the past couple of years, they had goaded Marian and Eugenia about their ages and unmarried state, even though they themselves were scarcely younger.

"Well," began Marian, the brightness in her green eyes belying the calmness of her voice, "Mr. Talbot accepted Mama's invitation to dine with us this Thursday. And he was very polite to Mama, and seemed to know just what to say." Willing her mind to move from Mr. Talbot to Eugenia, and realising that she had not yet asked after her friend's wellbeing, she enquired, "Are you quite ready to be married, other than our last dress fittings, that is?"

"Quite ready," answered Eugenia radiantly. "Are you still expecting me tomorrow?"

"Yes! I am hoping to find that I have now got the tucks to drape nicely. If the drape is right, then I have only the hem and skirt trim to finish."

"I do not know what I should have done without your expert needle and discerning taste, Marian. I should have shown up in my house dress and apron, I think!"

"Nonsense! I would never have allowed it," said Marian with a chuckle, giving Eugenia's arm a friendly squeeze before letting go.

Marian saw her friend was now distractedly looking up toward the church with shining eyes and a glowing smile. Marian guessed by the enviable flush of happiness that settled over Eugenia's face, that Eugenia's intended husband must be crossing the lawn to join them, and one quick glance told her that she was correct. Lawrence Trellaway was leisurely making his way toward them.

Marian nodded her head in greeting to the young man, and said cheerfully, "Good day, Mr. Trellaway. Eugenia and I were just discussing the wedding."

"Were you now?" He said with a mischievous smile, his eyes pleasantly crinkling up at the corners. "I thought you might be speaking of dresses!"

"Quite right! A most *particular* dress," teased Eugenia.

If it hadn't been Sunday, in the churchyard, with a ready audience, Mr. Trellaway's impassioned expression made Marian think that he might have kissed Eugenia indiscreetly then and there. But instead, he said to his bride-to-be, "Every strike of the church bell reminds me that the best of days will soon be here," and lifted Eugenia's hand and brushed her knuckles with a fleeting kiss.

Eugenia gave him a radiant smile, "Lawrie, Mr. Jennings' nephew was in church this morning. Were you introduced? For Marian says he is to dine with them later this week."

Lawrence shook his head thoughtfully. "I've not yet had the pleasure of his acquaintance." He paused and smiled tenderly at his betrothed. "However, my Love, I will go out of my way to seek his acquaintance, if it pleases you."

"Oh, it would please me greatly," coaxed Eugenia with a wink at Marian. "We need to see Marian comfortably and happily settled, and none of the swains in Cherrybrook are up to snuff."

Lawrence chuckled. "No, indeed? Very well, then, ladies. I will do my utmost to ferret the fellow out!"

Laughing, Eugenia gave Marian a quick hug and took Lawrie's arm to depart, casting over her shoulder her promise not to forget about her dress fitting the next day, and hopeful wishes for Marian's own happy future.

Marian hummed to herself as she put on her sewing apron, and dropped her scissors, pin case and pencil in the pocket.

When she heard a knock at the door, she opened it herself and invited Eugenia inside. Eugenia thrust a bouquet of fragrant pinks into Marian's hands and began talking as she lifted her skirts and stepped into the house. She followed Marian up the stairs and into her room.

"Papa has come into town with me and has dropped me off. Do you know where he is going?" Without giving Marian time to answer, Eugenia went on, "He is going to see Mr. Jennings! You know that the dear fellow is Papa's solicitor. You can be sure that I shall interrogate him when we are at supper tonight."

"You're *such* a friend, Eugenia. Now, do let me help you out of your morning dress and into your wedding gown."

Once Eugenia had slipped into the dress, Marian set to work, whirling around her, tucking in fabric here, and securing it there with pins.

"It really doesn't need much more adjusting," said Marian, cocking her head and looking critically at the fall of the fabric skirt. "Take a turn about the room, won't you?"

Eugenia did as she was asked, musing aloud, "I wish I had your head for details, Marian. I cannot imagine how it is that you make your own patterns! You seem to see the finished gown in your mind, and with only some quick sketches and a few measurements, here it is," she said softly, looking at herself in Marian's full-length mirror.

"Oh, it's such fun to sew for a wedding!" replied Marian with feeling. "I am honoured that you asked *me* of all people! You could have gone to a modista in Dorchester." She was so cast into the gloom by this thought that Eugenia was quick to reassure her.

"The best needles of Dorchester could have nothing on you," said Eugenia confidently. She smiled shrewdly, "Besides, you need to practise sewing wedding clothes. After all, it may not be long before you need to sew your own!"

Marian blushed mightily. "Stop. I insist. Why, we don't know anything yet about Mr. Talbot."

"*I* did not name a name! *You* have done it yourself," Eugenia burst out laughing. "But I won't breathe a word more about it. I promise."

Marian helped Eugenia out of the bridal confection, and into her everyday dress, then the two women went downstairs to take tea with the rest of the Lyle family.

Bonus Chapter Two

I t was Thursday, and there was much to be done before the Jennings and Mr. Talbot arrived. Perhaps in grander houses all the work and preparation for dinner guests would have been undertaken solely by servants, but in the Lyle home, there was just one cook, a kitchen girl, one manservant, and a part-time groundskeeper.

Marian spent the morning in her father's study and was now surreptitiously looking at the clock. The minutes and hours were passing with all the speed of a tired, and perhaps elderly, tortoise.

Marian sighed a little and tapped her fingers absent-mindedly on the desk. Before her were two open books and an inkwell, paper, and blotter. She turned in her chair to look at her father.

Reverend Lyle stood with his back to Marian. He was looking out a pair of tall, leaded glass windows that faced the lilacs and trees that separated the house from church. Marian knew her father claimed to do his best thinking while gazing at the spire of Holy Cross and over the treetops to the sky beyond.

His chin lifted. He was squinting off into that soft green and blue distance now. His hands were behind his back, and he rocked backwards and forwards on his heels. He smiled slightly and his mouth opened as though he were about to speak, but instead, he hesitated and looked up at the ceiling. Marian knew by his manner that he was on the cusp of elucidation, so she turned back to the desk, dipped the fountain pen, blotted it, and held the pen poised over the sheet of paper, ready for his dictation.

"Where was I, Mari?" Her father asked. She glanced up at him; his heavy brows were knitted in thought.

"Just now? She answered, "Why, nowhere, Papa. You said nothing."

"No... before." He gestured with his hand to a small stack of handwritten sheets in front of her.

Patiently, Marian reached for the topmost paper and read aloud, "'The practice of true faith proves its verity by resulting actions, 'spiritual fruit', the scriptures call it. In other words, one must pay strict attention to the phrase, 'practise of', for the action implied therein suggests that the best version of our faith is found in the doing of it. Fruit borne of practising selflessness, prudence, and hum ility.'"

"Ah!" he said. "Let us continue with that marvellous passage on acts of faith for the common man. Westford spoke so eloquently on this, that I fear I should be doing the topic an unforgivable injustice by not referring to his writing. Mari, do you remember where to find Westford's sermons? I seem to recall that you found it for me the last time I needed it."

Marian replied faintly, "I expect I can find it again. Let me see..." She had set the pen down and was in the middle of scooting the chair back from the writing desk when her father stopped her.

"I'm sorry, m'dear." her father said, studying her with concern. "You are biting your lip. Am I keeping you from something?"

Marian released her lip and lifted her gaze apologetically to his. "Today is Thursday." She waited for the significance of this statement to take effect, and when it did not, she went on. "Mr. and Mrs. Jennings and Mr. Talbot are joining us for dinner this evening."

As comprehension dawned on his face, Mr. Lyle broke into a smile. "That's right! I had completely forgotten. You must be needed by your mother. Fetch me that volume of sermons and be off with you. I shall be fine on my own for a while."

Marian's face lit up with anticipation and she smiled appreciatively at her father and then turned her attention to the bookshelves. She took a few steps to the tallest shelf to the right of the desk and ran her fingers along the spines until she came to a small, bright green book. She pulled it from the shelf, opened to the contents page and quickly scanned the headings. Ah! There they were, three homilies by Reverend T. Westford. She shut the small book triumphantly and returned to the desk.

"Here. I am setting the book here, Papa. It's green. If you check the table of contents, you will find the sermon that I think you are wanting." Her father was already back at the window, and she hovered near the desk, taking in the disarray. Sighing lightly, she quickly closed two open volumes and stacked them neatly one upon another, with the larger of two at the bottom. Then, with a glance at her father's back, she shook her head ruefully, swished the pen in a nearby cup of water, and dried the point gently with a rag set nearby for the purpose.

"I am going to help Mama now, but I will be happy to resume here with you tomorrow. Don't overwork yourself, Papa."

He turned and waved her off, "No, no! Of course, I shall not. See you at dinner."

Marian went out the door and shut it as quietly as she could, then she wiped her hands on her apron and hurried down the hall to look for her mother.

"There you are!" sang out Mrs. Lyle from the bottom of the stairs, her hands on her hips. "Your father let you go, did he? He remembered!"

"No, but he could see that I was not as content as usual, and when he asked me why, I reminded him that we are expecting guests. What remains to be done?"

"You and Esther choose the tablecloth and the serving dishes. Oh, bring in some cut flowers and set them out, won't you? Then," she said with a knowing smile, "I should think you'll need the remainder of the time to dress!"

Marian descended the stairs and followed her mother into the dining room. Once there she was left to her own devices.

"Esther!" called Marian. "Do come and lend me a hand."

The dining parlour was generously proportioned, for a vicar and his family must often be hospitable. And while the room was not especially elegant, it was well-maintained, and all the wood was polished and smelled of lemon and linseed oil. Marian crossed the room to a sideboard and opened the wide drawer which held the table clothes. Inside were three pressed, white damask clothes. She took one out and set it upon the edge of the walnut dining table and looked at it critically. "It will need another pressing. Perhaps Esther can-"

"Esther can what?" asked her sister, entering the room.

"There you are! Would you iron this or see if Martha will do it? Oh, and the napkins.... and before you go, help me lay out the dishes."

Esther and Marian pulled out and polished the silver pieces, and chose a couple of vases that looked especially lovely together.

"I do not see why Mr. Talbot has chosen you to care about, Marian," said Esther flatly as she pulled in her chin and peered critically at an elegantly-tooled, silver soup ladle. Marian knew her sister did not mean to be unkind. Like her, Esther tended to say what she thought to her family members without regard for mannerly trivialities.

Marian looked up from the silver tray she was cleaning. "I am not so sure he has. It must be far too early to assume any such thing."

"It is not that you aren't pretty," continued Esther, "but you will allow that you aren't the prettiest. He could have marched up to Eugenia and introduced himself. She has far more bloom than you have."

"She is engaged to Mr. Trellaway, and since they are in love, she is constantly blushing," said Marian testily.

"We might know that, but Mr. Talbot did not last Sunday."

"His uncle or aunt might have told him."

"Maybe. But then there are the Kents."

Marian put down the tray and rag at this, and stared in disbelief at her sister. "Of all of the miserable remarks!"

Esther put up her hand and blurted hastily, "You're right, Mari. I went too far. You are much sweeter and a little prettier than the Kents. Even if you are shy."

Marian's eyes widened and she took up her rag as if to swat at her sister, but did not. It was not in her nature. Instead, she giggled and Esther broke into laughter.

"Next time you think of such things," said Marian, whose face had grown serious again, "do me a favour and do not speak of it! Silly thoughts and assumptions only make me nervous. If you say one more word about Mr. Talbot, I shall be forced to hide in my room when he arrives."

Esther went off to the laundry to take care of the table linens, and Marian went out into the garden with the vases. She found the most perfect white roses and cornflowers that she could. After cutting them, she pinched off the bottom leaves, then, with a few sprigs of lavender and green herbs, she artfully arranged them in the vases. Satisfied with her floral arrangements, she carried the filled vases back into the dining parlour.

The sisters fitted the cloth to the table and Marian set one vase of blooms in the centre and the second on a sideboard. Finally, they laid the table with napkins, the silverware and the silver serving utensils. When they had finished, Esther and Marian agreed that the table and room looked as elegant as it ever had. They ought now to devote themselves to dressing.

Esther had helped Marian to dress and set the ringlets in her hair. At her sister's direction, she tied a narrow, yellow silk ribbon around Marian's pale blonde hair. Marian wore a cotton dress covered in small, yellow rosebuds. She had sewn it with fashionably dropped shoulders and a narrow, pointed waist, that flattered her small frame.

When Marian and Esther were ready, they went downstairs and Marian tried unsuccessfully to keep from looking out the window every few minutes. At last the clock chimed out the dinner hour and the Jennings and Mr. Talbot arrived in short order.

"Papa!" called Marian from the foot of the stairs as she crossed to the front hall. "Come and greet our guests!" She stood behind her mother and happily curtseyed and took hats and shawls, handing them to the housemaid.

Mr. Talbot was the personification of courtesy, waiting patiently behind the Jennings while her parents exchanged pleasantries with them.

Carlton Jennings was a solid man who looked the part of a reliable lawyer. He had a pleasant voice and a serious demeanour without being depressing. He had rather long, greying hair, a bit out of fashion now, and he wore it shaped in the style of old court wigs. Mrs. Jennings was not very tall, but she was wide. She wore an enormous hat, a snug pale green redingote and a false rump that padded her out at the hips. She reminded Marian of a bold pink peony in bloom, and her brightness and good humour did nothing to discourage the comparison.

Mr. Lyle was introduced to Mr. Talbot, and eagerly engaged the younger man in conversation. This distraction allowed Marian to take her time in observing Mr. Talbot.

Marian was struck by his carefree nature, from his sparkling brown eyes to his fashionable swoop of dark hair that pulled up at his forehead into a tidy wave. True, his teeth were not perfect, and he had a crooked smile, but that made him interesting and not at all unpleasant looking, she decided. Unlike his uncle and aunt, he was a good dresser. She wondered if he knew how closely the brown in his waistcoat matched his dark eyes, and how well the deep blue colour of his jacket suited him. He took obvious pains with his bow-tie cravat, and his trousers, shirt, vest, and jacket were of fine quality. While she watched, Mr. Talbot gently pulled at his cuffs and she saw the flash of a gemstone cufflink. When she glanced at his face again, she was shocked to see that he was smiling at her. Not only that, he winked!

Marian quickly looked away from Mr. Talbot in confusion. Nothing in her experience had prepared her for how to respond correctly to flirting. Was he flirting? Perhaps she did not understand his intentions. She inhaled sharply and turned her attention to Mrs. Jennings. Soon her mother suggested that they all adjourn to the dining parlour. Like a shepherdess, her mama pointed the way with one hand, and beckoned with the other. "Come in, won't you? Let us all be seated!"

Marian sat between her father and Esther. Directly across from her sat Mrs. Jennings, and to the right of that robust woman was Mr. Talbot. Marian tried to calm her pounding heart, for although Mr. Talbot was engaged with answering questions put to him by her mother from her place at the end of the table, he did spare her several discreet glances. He relaxed back in his chair when her mother wasn't looking, and shot Marian a smile over the rim of his wine glass. The slight raising of his dark eyebrows made her heart somersault.

Her mother had asked him to recount his history. How long was he here? What was he destined to do with himself?

"I must confess that I am fresh from school! Having read law for several years, I am desirous of becoming a barrister, but I am currently unable to remain in London for the correct introductions. It would seem I must proceed circumspectly." He glanced in Marian's direction. "I do not yet know how long I shall remain in Cherrybrook, but I find it a very fine little town indeed. It will be no punishment to stay here as long as my uncle can use my assistance."

"Tell us about your family, Mr. Talbot. Do you have a large family in...? I cannot call to mind where you told me you were from. I know that you told me last Sunday, but I seem to have forgotten."

Pinnset, Marian recited to herself.

"Pinnset," replied Mr. Talbot patiently. "Perhaps you have never been there? It is about a two hours' ride north and east."

The hitherto silent Mr. Jennings leaned forward and contributed, "My sister Alice, Jonas's mother, and I actually grew up in Dorchester, children of an attorney. It would seem that we Jennings are singularly unimaginative in our choice of profession." Here Mr. Jennings chuckled merrily. "When I went off to London to study, Alice married and moved to Pinnset with her husband."

Mrs. Lyle nodded and smiled at Mr. Jennings, and then addressed Jonas again. "Did you make acquaintances during your stay in London?"

"An individual with any particle of good breeding can and ought to make useful connections if living in London, and so I say, yes! I have several friends. I spent much time in the company of James Dollan of Slough and the Miles Duxsbury family, who visited London numerous times from their home in Weymouth. Now of course we are all scattered about, trying to make our way in the world and secure what fortunes we may."

"Are you Mrs. Talbot's eldest son or do you have brothers and sisters?"

"I am a second son," he gave an enigmatic smile, "but not the youngest. I have two younger brothers."

"Four sons and no daughters! What about your mother then, is she in good health?"

There was a brief pause and a hint of tension around his mouth as he answered, "My mother is in fine health. The best, in fact. She has my elder brother to look after her."

"And how about your younger brothers?"

"My brothers are easy enough to manage, young and of good temper. Henry is ten and two and Andrew is eight."

Mrs. Lyle sat back in her chair and pulled in her chin and, with a prim nod, took a spoonful of her soup. Marian relaxed her shoulders a little. Her mother had, apparently, been satisfied with his answers.

Marian was perfectly content to be quiet and listen, but soon she became aware that Mrs. Jennings was addressing her from across the table. Marian was a little flustered by this, and said, "I do apologise, ma'am. I did not hear you. Would you mind repeating your question?"

Mrs. Jennings chuckled and clucked, fanning herself in jest. She turned pointedly to Mr. Talbot and then looked back at Marian.

"I see you are dressed to the mark this evening. Such a pretty little rosebud print, too! Is that one of your recent sewing triumphs?"

"No." Marian stopped her spoon mid-bite. "That is... yes, I did make it myself, only not recently. My latest endeavour is the most challenging garment I have attempted by far; I am making a bridal gown for Miss Merritt. You know she and Mr. Trellaway are shortly to be wed."

"Really? My goodness! I should be terrified to attempt such a project on fabric as costly as that. No. I would leave it to an expert modista. Are you using a pattern?"

"I had a pattern for a very elegant ball gown that both Eugenia and I adored, and then I remembered having seen an illustration of a wedding dress with similar lines in a book at a shop. Once I got home that same day, I took up a pencil and set my memory to paper along with my estimates of the measurements. I am using my sketch combined with the pattern now to make the dress."

Mrs. Jennings tipped to her left, nearer Marian's father, and said, "Sir. your daughter is so clever with a needle, and so handy with numbers and figures, too? It is quite astounding."

"Thank you, Madam. Yes, we are very proud of her! She acts as my secretary and librarian whilst I write sermons. No one can remember a verse or a number more readily than she. I shall hate to see her go," and Reverend Lyle looked fondly at his eldest.

Marian felt herself colour and said in confusion, "I do not plan on going anywhere, Papa."

"No?" he teased. "We all intend for you to marry, do we not? If you do not, what will poor Esther do? She is waiting for you to go first, you know, and she is having rather a long wait of it." Here he laughed heartily, and Marian was mortified, realising that the rest of the dinner party had stopped talking and were looking toward the head of the table.

Her mother intervened from the foot of the table, "Reverend Lyle, I do not know what you have said, but poor Marian is as red as a beet. I pray you desist."

Marian was indeed blushing furiously; she could feel her flaming face. She looked down at her nearly empty bowl and hoped everyone would start up talking again, which they did almost at once. Her father reached over and patted her hand.

He said softly, "I am sorry, my dear. I forgot that a young man was present."

Perhaps to spare Marian from further mortification, Mr. Talbot stood quickly, the feet of his chair noisily scraping the floor and said, "I propose a toast to our host and hostess, their family and to the kindness of the people of Cherrybrook. May you prosper and please God."

There was a small burst of cheer, and everyone went back to talking and ignored the grateful Marian.

By the second course, she had fully recovered and was again engrossed in conversation.

Never was there a more jovial group, and the youngest Lyle, Michael, entered the dining room during dessert to see what was making them so merry. He had been persuaded to eat with the cook, Mrs. Barth, that evening so that the table would be even. Now he came creeping in, looking as though the promised extra helping of dessert in exchange for dining apart had not been such a terrific bargain after all.

When at last it was time for Mr. and Mrs. Jennings and Mr. Talbot to leave, Marian retrieved their hats and wraps and as she handed them out, she smiled broadly, She could not contain her honest pleasure. It had been such a diverting evening! Mr. Talbot was so very entertaining, and the Jennings were always a delightful pair.

When Marian shyly handed Mr. Talbot his hat, he brushed her fingers with his as he took it. She would have thought it an accident, but he smiled at her significantly and said, "I truly enjoyed your company." Then looking to see if he were unobserved, he kissed his finger that had grazed hers- as though it were a sacred thing and said sotto voce, "Do you know, Miss Lyle? I think I would like to host a small party and invite you, your sister, and any friends that you care to recommend. I shall ask you to play hostess, for I understand you have great powers of organisation. I confess, even though I practise law, organisation has never been a credit to me. Shall we plan something, perhaps, around four weeks from today?"

Marian did not know what to say. She was flattered but was not at all sure it was proper. With brows creased in thought and with a timid smile, she said, "Once you have asked permission of your aunt and uncle, and received their approval, I shall be happy to lend my assistance."

"Along with your good character, is it then?" he asked with a low chuckle.

Marian smiled at this and rejoined cleverly, "If you do not have enough of your own good character, I shall have to withdraw my offer, Mr. Talbot."

As the Jennings were stepping out the front door, he lowered his voice even further and said, "I shall count each day a loss until I next see you. Goodnight, Miss Lyle."

And with that, he was gone. He was out the door and walking alongside his uncle in a trice.

Read the whole story! Visit https://charlottebrothers author.com to find your preferred book vendor.

Also by Charlotte Brothers

"A Year in Cherrybrook' is a book series of sweet late Regency/early Victorian era romances. Four light-hearted, character-driven love stories take place in spring, summer, autumn and winter in or around the fictitious English country village of Cherrybrook. They may be read in order or as stand-alone stories.

A FAIR-WEATHER FRIEND | Book Two: Summer
Is the wrong brother the right man?
Miss Marian Lyle knows what to do with a column of figures or a garment to sew, but a charming newcomer has her in a muddle!

A BIRD IN THE HAND | Book Three: Autumn
Art, Fate, and Forbidden Love
A handsome new vicar and the local baron's daughter: art brought them together, but will fate pull them apart?

TIME WILL TELL | Book Four: Winter
Matchmaking gone wrong

Mrs. Lavinia Fitzroy is just the woman to find widowed Dr. Rafe Reynolds a wife. She's audacious, well-connected and entirely uninterested in marriage for herself!

126